HAUNTING *you*

Molly Zenk

USA Today Bestselling Author

Appropriate for Teens, Intriguing to Adults

Immortal Works LLC
1505 Glenrose Drive
Salt Lake City, Utah 84104
Tel: (385) 202-0116

Cover Art by Ashley Literski
http://strangedevotion.wixsite.com/strangedesigns

ISBN 978-1-7339085-9-7 (Paperback)
ASIN B081446JYT (Kindle Edition)

Haunting, Colorado
Present Day

I dream to escape.

I know what people must think. Everyone assumes I live a charmed life. Only child of the headmaster of an exclusive boarding school. Girlfriend to the school sports hero. Straight-A student. Who doesn't want all that?

Me.

Sometimes, it feels like I'm on the outside looking in. I go through the motions of my life, but there's no connection there. There's no spark to let me know I'm doing more than just breathing air. I'm a ghost.

At least, I feel like one. That's why I need to escape. In my dreams, I'm not Meredith. I'm someone else. Someone named Mercy. Ever since Mom died, I've been Meredith by day and Mercy at night.

It haunts me. It plays out like a movie in my head. I'm me, but I'm not me. I'm wearing fancy gowns and dancing at balls that look like leftover sets from some costume drama on PBS. People call me "Mercy," and I respond as if I'm her. When I wake up, I take longer and longer to remember I'm Meredith, not Mercy. I'm not that girl in the fancy gown dancing the night away. I'm not that girl who runs off to meet up with her secret lover, Nate.

Though I wish I were.

My phone buzzes, breaking the spell from the latest dream. I pull it toward me from the nightstand next to my bed without even sitting up and check the caller. Jay. Looks like I missed ten texts from him. "Missed" might be the wrong word. "Ignored" is better. His overprotectiveness is one reason I need to escape.

"You best answer that." My friend Abigail appears out of nowhere. "Mr. Jay is not someone you should ignore."

"You sound like my dad." I sit up in bed. I don't usually nap at three in the afternoon, but I needed an escape and it gives me a ready-made excuse to Jay. I've become a master of excuses—but I wish I could tell the truth about the dreams sometime to someone, anyone. My fingers fly over my qwerty keyboard as I type *sorry, sleeping* into the text box. I hit send, not even bothering to read any of the messages I missed.

I lie back down but keep my eyes open to watch Abigail putter around my dorm room. She's wearing one of those old-fashioned maid outfits like the tourists get excited over at the Old-Time Photo store on St. Michael Street. Even her hair is done up in a low Gibson-girl roll at the nape of her neck, something that hasn't been popular since this side of 1900. Everything about Abigail seems stuck in the past. Not that it's a bad thing, but I think when you live in a place with so much history, some people forget that history is over and done with, you know? It's time to move on. And then, some forget the moving on part. Like Abigail.

"You know you don't have to clean up, right?" I remind her. "It's not, like, your job anymore."

"Old habits die hard, miss."

She fluffs my pillow, straightens my bedspread, and runs a white rag across the mantel of my fireplace. It's a real fireplace, leftover from the time the school was a Victorian hotel. It, like a lot of the leftover opulence, is just for show. The headmaster (also known as my dad) wouldn't trust us with fire. He doesn't even trust us with inter-dorm visitation. That's just asking for trouble. Not that I'd get in trouble—being labeled the "good girl" has its perks when your dad all but lets you raise yourself—but I know plenty of people that would.

"You don't have to do that, either," I say.

Abigail looks up and blinks her wide, dark eyes at me. "Do what, miss?"

"Call me 'miss.' I know you're just being polite, Abigail, but I—" I wave a hand to find words that won't make me sound like I'm putting down how her parents raised her. I need to start thinking things through instead of saying the first thought that pops into my head. Not that I ever say the first thought that pops into my head anyway— especially around Abigail, who is old-fashioned about how girls our age should talk and act. I've trained myself to put everyone else's needs before my own. It's easier to blend in when everyone trusts you to do the right thing.

"What else should I call you, miss?" Abigail asks.

"I know you think because I'm the headmaster's daughter that makes me elite or something, but I don't feel that way," I say. "I'm not any different from anyone else just because Dad started this school. I don't think we need to stand on formally. I mean, formality. We can just be cool. No need to call me 'miss.' I'm Meredith. Just call me Meredith."

Abigail's whole body relaxes as if my words give her permission to just be a girl instead of Mayor of Formal Town. She glides across the room and settles onto the edge of my bed. At first, she doesn't seem to know what to do with her hands when they're not cleaning something. She settles on clasping and unclasping them in her lap.

I motion at her hands. "Still nervous?"

"I have a job to do," she replies.

I shake my head. "Not anymore. Why don't we talk? You're my age, right? Sixteen?"

Abigail bites her lower lip as if unsure if she should talk to me or not before nodding. "Yes, miss—I mean, Meredith."

"Then let's do what normal sixteen-year-old girls do. Let's gossip."

Abigail laughs. I bet she hasn't had a good gossip session in years and years. I open my mouth to ask when was the last time she talked to someone besides me before deciding to change the topic to the number one interest to girls throughout history --Boys.

"So, Jay is kind of a pain. I mean, I know we're, like, together, but he seriously signed up for all the same classes as me. I mean, who does that? Especially when they're trying to graduate on time."

Abigail smiles and leans back on the bed, melting into the wall a little. "Jay is *so* handsome. You're very fortunate he is your fellow."

I snort. "Sometimes, I think handsome is about all Jay has going for him."

"And that's a problem?" Abigail furrows her brow, confused.

"Well, not usually, but it can be." I glance across the room to my framed picture of me, Mom, and Dad. It was our only all-together pro shot, taken three years ago right before what I call The Night That Changed Everything. The night before I first had the Mercy dreams. "No matter how frustrating Jay can be now, he has helped me through a lot these last three years. I got to give him credit for that."

I'm not sure if Abigail answers or not. I'm too lost in my own thoughts. That night—The Night That Changed Everything—is as clear in my mind as if it happened yesterday instead of three years ago. One minute Mom, Dad, and I are driving along a mountain switchback singing Christmas carols, the next we're skidding off the cliff. The only things that stopped us were pine trees and luck. Jay was there for me when all Dad wanted to do was ignore the grief and throw all his time and energy into the school. Sometimes I feel I lost both my parents that night. Yet another reason to escape my supposedly perfect life.

The lights flicker. Abigail appears to flicker with them. "Oh, no," she whispers. "It's happening again."

The "again" gives me a jolt of something I can't quite name. Vertigo? Déjà vu? I'm not sure what it is, but one minute I swear it feels like I'm dancing under the bright candlelight of the chandeliers in the grand-ballroom-turned-dining-hall, wearing a fancy blue dress and old-fashioned shoes; the next, I'm back in my room still sitting on my bed.

Abigail stands. "I need to go. I need to help. I can't let it end like last time. I can't."

Before I can stop her, Abigail walks through the door. I don't mean she opens the door and then walks through it. I mean she literally walks through the door. Abigail, like so many others in this hotel-turned-school, is dead. To someone like me who can see and hear ghosts after the accident, she looks as solid and real as anyone going to school here. Sure, she wears turn-of-the-century clothes and isn't exactly tied to our physical laws—what with sitting on my bed one minute and walking through the door the next—but Abigail and all the others are not just a fun story to scare tourists with. To me she's real. I found out within hours after the accident that ghosts can exert enough energy to move physical objects and touch the living. (There's a crazy amount of spirits hanging around a hospital.) That shivery feeling you get when no one else is around? That's a ghost reaching out. If I tried to touch one in return, my hand would go right through them.

The former hotel staff aren't stuck in our realm; they just hang around the living and continue their previous earthly duties. Having a ghost staff is not something Dad puts in the brochure, just like having a daughter that talks to the dead after getting a nasty concussion during The Night That Changed Everything is something he advertises. I keep quiet about that too. As far as I know, I'm the only one on campus who can see and hear our ghost companions. If anyone else around here can, they're being low-key about it, which, if you ask me, is a smart move. Standing out is not always a good thing. Who wants the label of freak? The one ghost I want to show up—Mom—never has. I wish I knew why.

I hear a commotion in the hallway that sounds like what happens when the boys pull the fire alarm at night, hoping to catch girls in the shower and send them out into the courtyard clad in nothing but a towel. When it feels like you're one of the last schools in creation that sticks to the no-inter-dorm-visitation rule, you get your thrills where you can find them. Abigail left in a hurry with the bonus of being all cryptic. The fire alarm is not blaring now, so what else is going on?

I stick my head out my door and watch the other girls on my floor stream past. "Hey, what's going on?" I call to the first girl that stops to look my direction. I recognize her as a freshman named Patrice. If there was drama, Patrice was front and center. She liked to say she knew whoever was involved or was wherever the event happened. I think it made her feel important.

"There's been an accident," Patrice says.

"What kind?"

"Some kid on a campus tour fell over the rotunda rail. I heard it's that kid from Twin Lakes. You know, the one who lost his parents in that boating accident last month?" Gossip—whether it's true or not—travels fast around campus. Patrice's friend looks a little too gleeful at the thought of some epic accident happening just a couple flights of stairs below us. I bet she was already imagining walking into a live news shot or tweeting about how she was there when the kid fell. She turns to her friend, already forgetting me. "Hey, do you think if we hurry downstairs, we can be on the news? I bet I can cry on cue. It'll be awesome."

She's out of question range. I can't get any more details like if the boy from Twin Lakes was just clumsy or pushed by a human or ghost. Asking about the ghost part would violate my policy of never, ever talking about ghosts or the fact I can hear and see them, but there's got to be a reason that right before the accident Abigail spazzed out and disappeared. Maybe the boy's fall is related somehow. There's only one way to find out. I need to go downstairs too.

I only take enough time to pull my hair into a low ponytail and squirm into shoes before I follow the crowd down the three flights of stairs toward the lobby.

"I saw the guy do a swan dive over the rail," one girl says, gossiping to her friends, relishing the gruesome details of the accident. Maybe Dad should let up on some of his strict rules if this is what my classmates do for entertainment now. The gossipy girl waited until there was a crowd around her before continuing her I-was-there story. I bet her I-was-there story will turn into Patrice's I-was-there story before the day is out. "One minute it's 'to your left is the stained-glass window commissioned by Charles Haunting himself,' the next minute it's one story down straight into the rotunda tile."

"Did he jump or fall?" I ask, but no one is listening. They're too wrapped up in each other's dramatic re-creations to hear or care about me. I may be the headmaster's daughter, but I pride myself on being as invisible as possible. Invisible helps me keep my secret close, but it's not the greatest when I want answers. Like now. I open my mouth to ask my question again. The group of girls keeps right on gossiping, without a second thought or glance my direction.

"Do you think they've cleaned up all the blood yet?" the ringleader's friend gasps.

"Oooh, let's go check," the ringleader squeals as if her friend suggested looking at fuzzy kittens to adopt instead of checking out a potential crime scene. "If he survives, I bet Headmaster Monroe will give him boatloads of scholarship money to not sue him."

"Remind me to jump off the rotunda the next time tuition is due."

"I hope the guy is hot."

"No one is hot after doing a face-plant into old tile."

"Good one."

The girls give each other a high five before I lose them and their conversation in the crowd gathered in the rotunda around the accident victim. By any normal standards, this should be a big deal, not a photo op. Boys don't fall off of rotunda balconies every day—even in Haunting, which is known for its "unusual occurrences." The girls from my dorm floor shouldn't be crowded around a potential crime scene hoping reporters ask them questions. They should give the paramedics space to work. They should be worried about the boy. I don't even know him and my heart is pounding so fast it feels like it's going to jump out of my chest. I know we're pretty sheltered since we live in our own little world at boarding school, but when did *this* become entertainment? When did hoping to catch a glimpse of a bruised and bloodied boy become something to do on a Friday afternoon? I shudder. If Dad didn't insist I attend his little brainchild Haunting Academy, I'd be looking for a new school pronto.

I maneuver my way to the front of the crowd to try to get a clear look of the boy from Twin Lakes. He looks close to my age, but I can't be sure since he's got blood all over his face. He's lying on one of those pop-up gurney beds as the EMTs work on him, eyes closed, mouth parted, and dark hair matted to his face. I can't tell if he's breathing or not. The world feels like it's tilting—spinning—like how I felt in my room when Abigail said something was happening again. The only difference is, this time, instead of feeling like I'm dancing under the chandeliers in the grand-ballroom-turned-dining-hall, I'm walking along the beach. I feel the sand under my feet, but something —no, not something—*someone* is not right.

Fear like I've never known grips me as I push my way through the gathering crowd of curious students, worried teachers, and random tourists. No one tries to stop me or pull me back or tell me I don't belong as I rush to the boy's side. I belong there. If there's one thing I've ever been sure of in my entire life, it's that I belong at this boy's side, right here, right now.

"No, please, no," I whisper as I brush his dark hair away from his face. I don't care about the blood or bruises or anything but him living. "Nate. Please, no. Don't leave me. Don't leave me."

The boy's eyes flutter open, and he takes a breath deep enough to make his chest rise before that same breath hisses out in pain. "Mercy?"

"I'm here, Nate." Words tumble out before I can stop them or have time to wonder why I'm calling him Nate—the same name as Mercy's secret boyfriend in my dreams. I smooth his dark hair back and kiss his cold forehead. "I'm here."

They're getting ready to take Nate away, and I can't let that happen. I don't even know if his name *is* Nate, but that's what I called him, so I'm going with that until I know otherwise. His hand is still in mine, holding on so tight that both our knuckles are white.

"Miss, what is your relationship to the victim?"

I jump, startled to remember we're not the only two people in the rotunda. One of the EMTs is looking at me.

"Um, relationship?" I ask.

"Sister? Girlfriend?" He flips open a little notebook, poised and ready to write everything I say. "We need to load him up into the ambulance, and we can't take you along unless you're related."

I smooth the boy's dark hair away from his forehead. His face is surprisingly cut- and bruise-free from the fall. I'm no doctor, but it looks like he took the brunt of the injuries to his ribs and left side. His breath wheezes and catches as it tries to maintain a rhythm akin to normal. My eyes fill up with tears for a boy I just met and know nothing about. Or do I?

I get that prickly hair-standing-on-end feeling that means a ghost is near. I look up to the scene of the fall. Abigail leans over the wooden, waist-high railing. "Go with him," she says.

If I answer her, I'll be the crazy girl talking out loud to herself with a death grip on the hand of a boy she doesn't know. It would only take one person in the crowd to pay attention to me for once for *that* rumor to spread. Instead, I shake my head just enough for Abigail to know I heard her and mouth, "How?"

"Think of something." Abigail shimmers in her earnestness. "Anything—just don't leave him. Go with him. He needs you."

The thing is, I'm the world's worst liar. If you want to clean up at cards, play poker with me. Rather than work on my poker face, I gave up any attempts at lying while growing up and decided it was easier to fall into the "good girl" role. It didn't help that I had no siblings to blame anything on. What was Abigail thinking asking me to lie my way into the boy's ambulance now? I give her an *okay, it's your funeral* look before opening my mouth.

"I'm his fiancé," I tell the EMTs. "Or-or, I would be. He didn't have time to propose. I was on my way to meet him when the accident happened."

What was that? I resist the urge to clamp my hands over my mouth. It's almost like the words belong to someone else. Someone who is way better at spinning stories than I am. The best part is, the EMT buys it hook, line, and sinker. I glance up at Abigail, who grins at me before disappearing.

"Do you know anyone else we can call to tell about the accident?" the first EMT asks.

I shake my head. "No. Sorry. There's just me."

I glance around the crowd, remembering where I'm at. I hope to hell my little performance piece doesn't get back to Jay. Things are awkward between us already (at least on my part). I don't need to explain why I made up a story about being engaged to someone else so I could ride along to the hospital. I flick my gaze around the crowd to find someone I think I can trust. In a room full of Patrice wannabes, I see Ritzi Carmichael. She's standing close to Nate, looking at him the same way I was a few minutes ago—like she knows him from somewhere. She blinks hard and shakes herself out of wherever she mentally ran off to. When she looks up, she sees me, and I motion for her to come closer. Ritzi lives in the dorm next to me and we share a bathroom. You learn a lot about a person when you share a bathroom. I can trust her.

"Ritzi, don't tell Jay I'm riding along to the hospital," I say.

She plays along. "Tell Jay what?"

"And let my dad know I'll be back when I can, okay? If anyone else asks, I'm just helping out the EMTs. I know more about the school than anyone else."

Ritzi gives me a salute. "Promise to tell me everything when you can! Patrice will have a fit if I know something before she does."

"I will!" I yell as the EMTs usher Nate and me out of the room and into the waiting ambulance.

THERE'S a whirlwind of commotion as we arrive at the hospital. I stay focused and single-minded as I follow the gurney. Abigail's words echo in my head: *Go with him. He needs you. Don't leave him.* My little stunt at school gave me a front row seat to his care I don't deserve, but I need to figure out why. Why is he so familiar? Why did I call him Nate? Why did he call me Mercy? Why did I hyperventilate at the thought of losing him? There's way, way too many whys and not enough answers.

I tune in and listen as the EMT rattles off the details of the accident.

"Sixteen-year-old male, Nathan Vale, fell a single story over a balcony onto marble tile. The extent of the injuries appears to be cracked ribs, facial lacerations, left dislocated shoulder, and bruising. I recommend an MRI to rule out internal damage. This is—" he motions at me— "his fiancée."

"Meredith," I supply. "Meredith Monroe."

"We'll take it from here, Miss Monroe," a female doctor says as they wheel him away before I can say anything else. That's it. He's gone as suddenly as he appeared.

I find a chair in the waiting room and sit down to do what the room wants me to do—wait. And I think. Nathan. His name is Nathan. Nathan Vale. Not Nate, just like my name is Meredith, not Mercy. I have plenty of time to run those words—*Nathan Vale*—over and over in my head while I wait for an update on his condition. I hope they don't think to check my shoddy cover story. Now I think of it, it sounds like something straight out of a 1990s romantic comedy. Except no one's laughing—especially if they find out it's not the truth, which it definitely is not. I never saw the guy before today.

At least, not while I've been awake.

I fidget with the Claddagh ring on my right hand. It's a simple silver design, nothing flashy, which is weird considering Jay, the master of flashy, over-the-top gestures, gave it to me. I've always liked that the crown, heart, and hands represent loyalty, love, and friendship. If the heart is turned in toward your body, it means you're in a relationship. I remember the night he gave it to me, I tried to wear it out, and he corrected me. "No," he'd said, slipping it off and turning it around, "you wear it this way. It means you're my girl, Mer. You'll always be my girl." Now I'm in a hospital chasing a stranger. How did I get to this point?

"Are you Nathan Vale's fiancée?"

A nurse is hovering near me with a clipboard. Good. No one checked my cover story. To the hospital staff, I'm still a fiancée instead of a complete stranger.

I stand, hoping I look the part of concerned fiancée or near-fiancée, depending on if you believed the "he would propose but didn't get the chance" story I fed the EMTs. "Yes, that's me. Is Nathan going to be all right? Can I see him?"

She nods. "Yes, and yes. Follow me, please. He's asking to see you too."

Chapter 3

Nathan looks up at me through his dark bangs after I close the door and take several staggering steps toward his bed. Despite whatever you want to call what passed between us earlier, right now is awkward. Really, really awkward. There're a million and two things I want to say, but not one comes to mind when I'm face-to-face with a wide-awake Nathan and able to say them.

"So, um, what am I supposed to call you?" he asks. "I want to say Mercy, but I know that's wrong, even though it feels right somehow."

I find the chair closest to Nathan's bed and sit down. "If anyone at the hospital asks, I'm your fake fiancée." I try to laugh, but no sound comes out. "It was the only thing I could say to get permission to ride along in the ambulance. Family only, so I became family."

Nathan watches me, but I feel he's actually seeing me and trying to figure me out, unlike Jay, who seems more into watching everyone else watch me so he can figure out who he needs to threaten for honing in on his trophy girlfriend. Not that I consider myself a good catch, but I *am* the headmaster's daughter. That holds a lot of clout when you want to get something done or have someone look the other way on campus.

"I'd like to know your name." Nathan reaches out a hand to me. "It'll make our sham hospital engagement more believable if I know what to call you."

I take his hand, careful not to jostle the IV taped to the top. "I'm Meredith."

He closes his eyes, face pale beneath the bruises, before nodding. "I'm Nathan, but you probably already knew that."

"I only know what the paramedics said. I know nothing else about you." I let go of Nathan's hand a moment to add an extra pillow behind his back before offering him a glass of ice chips. Nathan takes the glass and my hand again. "All I know is you fell, and I felt compelled to come up with a crazy story to get in that ambulance with you. I'm horrible at lying, by the way. I don't know how I could manage that Oscar-worthy story, but I did, and here am I."

"Here we are." Nathan cracks an eye open and motions to the space between us. "Like it or not, we're in this together now. Did I at least get you a good fake engagement ring?" He smiles, and I get that weird, tilting déjà vu feeling again. I see my bare feet running across the sand at Lake Menton near the school toward I'm not sure what. Or who.

I shake my head to snap myself out of the daydream or vision or whatever I'm supposed to call it. I need to answer Nathan. "I don't know. You fell over the railing before you had the chance to give me a ring."

He grimaces. "I think I like your fake version of events better than the real one."

"So, what happened up there?" I ask. "Do you remember?"

"I remember the tour," Nathan says. "I was looking at the cherubs and flower carvings on the banister when I heard my name." He frowns. "At least I thought it was my name. I heard a girl call 'Nate.' When I went to look over the rail down to the rotunda to see if she was down there, someone pushed me."

"Or something."

I didn't mean to just lay the paranormal entity possibility out there like that, but I did, and I can't take it back now. I know people like to talk about Haunting, Colorado, and the school, especially. It's big business. There're books and TV shows and even a movie about the paranormal activity in town. Dad's stance is the school is not and never has been haunted. I think if he were to just embrace the past instead of running from it, there would at least be a chance the living and dead could coexist with a little less restless energy in town and especially on campus. Still, if I told Dad what I think, he wouldn't want to listen. The only person Dad listens to is himself.

Nathan's dark brow forms a deep V in the middle of his forehead as he processes the meaning behind my two simple words. "Are the stories about this place really true? I thought calling the school Haunting Academy was just a wordplay on the town name. Is there, uh, more to it than that?"

"If you stay here long enough, you'll see," I say. "Everyone does, even if they write it off as a trick of the light or their imagination. Everything you've heard or seen on TV about Haunting is most likely true."

"And it all centers on the school?"

I make a so-so gesture with the hand not holding on to his. "Kind of. The school building used to be a hotel in a gold-mines-turned-resort town. There's a lot of unsettled history here. Unsettled history means unsettled energy. I'm a little surprised we haven't had more 'accidents' over the years." I bite down on my lower lip before adding, "Just be careful, okay?"

Nathan struggles to sit up higher in bed. "You should have warned me yesterday."

I frown. How hard did he hit his head? "I didn't know you yesterday."

"No, not yesterday-yesterday," he says. "When the school was a hotel yesterday."

I pull my hand free of his. It's shaking. "What are you talking about?"

"I've been having dreams that—no matter what I do—won't leave me alone," Nathan begins. "It's like playing a song on repeat. I even wake up and fall back asleep, and the dream starts up right where I left off. In the dream, I'm me, but I'm not me. I'm in love with a girl, but there's something standing in the way. I'm not sure what. A boyfriend or dad or something keeping us apart. We plan to be together but..." He trails off, lost in thought, before shaking his head. "I don't know what happens next. It gets kind of blurry. Maybe I'm not supposed to know, or maybe I need someone else along before I can find out more."

"Is that why you came here?" I ask. "Because of the dreams?"

"Yes, and no."

I pinch the bridge of my nose with my thumb and index finger. "You'll have to do better than that for an answer, Nate."

"Nathan," he corrects. "I'm not Nate. Not anymore at least, just like you're not Mercy anymore. You're Meredith. We're us, and they're them, but we might have been them. At least that's what I think the dreams are telling me."

I make a point not to look at Nathan, because if I look at his eager, sincere face, I'll believe him about the dreams and everything else, and I don't think I'm ready to do that yet. Instead, I play it off as a joke. It's the only thing I can think to do. "Are you sure you didn't hit your head harder than the doctor thought?"

"The dreams led me back here, Meredith," Nathan insists. "They led me back to you."

The hospital gave me a coupon for a free bus ride back to campus. I considered calling Jay to pick me up so I could avoid the meandering public transportation route home, but that would mean more lying. He'd ask too many questions that I didn't have answers for right now. Calling Dad was a big no, too. He didn't like me going off campus without Jay to "protect me." It wasn't an official Dad rule, but enough of one that I didn't want him to know I broke it. Ritzi didn't have a car, or I'd call her. Bus ride it is.

"We'll call you when your fiancée is ready to go home," the front desk nurse says as I'm on my way out. "If all the scans come back clean, he might be discharged tomorrow."

It takes me a second to realize she's talking to me. "Uh, thanks. I appreciate you guys taking care of him."

She smiles. "You'll have to show us your ring once he does get a chance to propose."

I twist the Claddagh ring on my finger. I hope I don't look as guilty as I feel. "Sure. Thanks again." I book it out the sliding glass doors before she asks more questions. I'm tired of questions. I'm tired of lies. I just want to go home.

I RECEIVE the call he's ready to be picked up the next morning.

I stare down at my phone after I hang up with the hospital receptionist. Nathan is ready to be discharged, and I'm the one they expect to pick him up. How am I supposed to get back there without Dad or Jay finding out my cover story to get into Nathan's hospital room yesterday?

"Meredith, sweetie, it's a phone, not a bomb," Dad says when he looks up from completing Nathan's amazing admissions and financial aid package and notices me staring at my phone. "What's wrong?"

"That was the hospital," I say. "They called me to say Nathan's ready to be discharged."

"And they called you?" He raises his eyebrow, but I'm lucky that a life spent in I-cannot-tell-a-lie-ville means he doesn't get suspicious of me now.

"I guess they put me down as his contact person." This not-telling-the-full-truth thing was getting easier. Maybe all I needed was a little practice or a good reason not to tell the full truth. "Can you take me to the hospital to pick him up?"

Dad motions at his paperwork. "Sorry, sweetie, I need to finish this up. Why not take the bus?"

I scrunch up my face and stick out my tongue. It's the face Mom always used to warn me about it getting stuck that way. "Busing is cruel and unusual punishment for someone with bruised ribs, Dad. What else do you got?"

"What about Jay?"

Jay. Why didn't I think of Jay? He has a car, and ski team practice is finished by now. I lean over Dad's oversized wooden desk and give him a peck on the cheek. "Thanks for the idea, Dad." I wave and head out the door before he can question why I didn't think to ask my boyfriend for a ride.

I pull out my phone again to text Jay.

Me: *Can't wait to see you.*

Jay: *Same place, same time.*

I'm grateful Jay and I always do brunch after Saturday ski practice. Me hanging around outside the boys' locker room in the athletic department looks less suspicious that way. Me asking Jay for a little pre-brunch detour to spring Nathan from the hospital will come across better too. I wait in my usual spot until Jay emerges, freshly showered and with his blond hair slicked back.

"Hey, babe." He leans over and kisses me on the mouth. It's a we're-in-a-public-place, how-you-doing kiss versus a get-a-room kiss. Jay, to his credit, is very patient with me when even I don't think he should be after two years of dating. I guess he has a lot of distractions with school and sports that figuring out ways to get me out of my clothes ranks low on his to-do list. Mom would call that being a gentleman, so I'll go with that theory over some other ones people come up with—like cheating on me or just not interested.

"Hey, back." I lean into him for a moment. He smells like soap and muscle rub. "How was practice?"

Jay shrugs. "Could be better. Some of our alternates quit."

"Sorry." I remember to be a supportive girlfriend instead of leading with what I really want to ask him. "I know how much the team means to you."

Jay shrugs again. "We'll get through it." His eyes narrow, noticing my jitterier-than-normal tick. I've been spinning my Claddagh ring around on my finger so much even I expect it to fly off. He motions at my hands. "What gives? If you have something to say, just say it, Meredith."

I get right to the point since he told me to. "Do you remember the transfer student that had the accident yesterday? Nathan? Nathan Vale?"

"Was he the reason you weren't answering my texts yesterday?"

Jay's expression darkens before he's back to being confident, unruffled Jay. "What about him?"

"You're right. I did spend some time with Nathan yesterday." I go for the truth. With my track record for rotten lying, it's easier. "The hospital staff thought we were related, so they let me hang out in his room to make sure he was okay. If he hadn't been touring Dad's school, he wouldn't be in the hospital in the first place, you know?" I tuck my hair behind my ear and take a breath. Time to get to the favor-part of the conversation. "Well, he's being discharged from the hospital this morning and needs a ride to campus. Dad suggested I enlist your help. I know we always do brunch, but this is important too. What do you say? Up for an adventure?"

"With you?" Jay grins, his bad mood vanishing as quickly as it came. "Any day."

He slings an arm around my shoulders, and we walk together to his car. I lean against him, reminding myself I need to be a better girlfriend. When Mom died, I locked my emotions down so deep that I didn't think I or anyone else could ever dig them up again. While Dad withdrew to throw himself into his work, Jay showered me with patience. He hasn't unlocked my full pre-accident emotions yet, but he has scratched the surface. I owe him for bringing me back around. I owe him for making me see there is a lot of life left to live. No matter how many late nights we've stayed up talking, though, I've never once mentioned the concussion knocking loose my sixth sense. That's my secret. I don't know if there's anyone I can trust with that.

We drive to the hospital in silence, content to just be near each other. I like quiet moments like this when I don't have to fill it up with talk. I wish every day could be like this.

Nathan is sitting in a wheelchair in the lobby, dressed in the same clothes he was wearing yesterday. He holds up a handful of paperwork when he sees me.

"Thanks for coming. They let me sign myself out once the doctor gave the all clear. Emancipated minor perk. They're making me ride in the wheelchair to the car, though."

"Nathan, Jay. Jay, Nathan." I introduce my boyfriend to my I-don't-know-what as fast as possible. "Dad texted me." I hold up my phone as proof. "Nathan, if you accept Dad's financial aid package, he says Jay will be your new roommate." That's about the worst idea I've ever heard, but what Dad says goes. "Who's ready to go back to campus?" I babble on. "I know I am."

"Are you Meredith's brother?" Nathan asks, which, come to think of it, is an honest mistake, considering Jay and I do look alike in a blond-haired, blue-eyed Nordic kind of way.

"Hardly," Jay laughs. "I'm her boyfriend. Going on two years, right, Mer?"

I just smile and nod because that's what Jay expects from his quiet, complacent, no-waves good girl. Even if that's not me deep down, even if I want to break out of the box I've put myself in since Mom died, it's just easier to play the part. It's familiar. Sometimes it's easier to stick with what you know instead of going with the unknown.

"Jay, why don't you, uh, grab the car. I'll push Nathan," I say. The sooner we get this sure-to-be-awkward drive home over with, the better.

"Sure, babe." Jay leans over and kisses the top of my head before loping off into the parking lot in search of his red Camaro.

Nathan cranes his neck around to look at me. "Boyfriend? Why didn't you tell me you had a boyfriend?"

"You didn't ask."

"I'm asking now."

"I didn't think it was important."

"Not important?" Nathan grimaces, and I can't tell if my lackadaisical attitude toward boyfriend status updates or his bruised ribs are bothering him. Or maybe both. "What else did you gloss over as 'not important' yesterday when we were talking all open and honest? I thought we had a connection, Meredith. I did. Now I don't know anymore."

"That's the point, Nathan." The words come out harsher than I mean for them to. "You don't know me. You may think you do, but you don't. You have this idea in your head of what I'm supposed to be like based on some dreams, but that's not me. That's a fantasy."

Nathan shakes his head. "That's not true. I won't believe that."

I've been too harsh. I know I have. I've hidden behind my layers of hurt and scars from Mom's death and lashed out at one person who definitely does not deserve it. If I'm being honest with myself, I'm scared. I'm scared of the connection I feel with Nathan. I'm scared of the pull. I'm scared of how that will mess up the organized life I've built up since the accident. It's easier to go with the flow than make waves. If I follow where this connection with Nathan leads me, I can almost guarantee it will make waves. It will be messy. It will wake me up and make me feel alive. Do I want that? I don't know, but I do know I shouldn't have snapped at him.

"Look, I'm sorry I said all that," I say. "If you want to get to know me, get to know me, but as the real me and not the fantasy, okay?"

Nathan smiles at me as Jay pulls up in the car. "Deal."

I crawl into the back seat next to Jay's ski gear to give Nathan more room to stretch out in the front. As we drive toward campus, I allow myself to think about the possibility of Nathan's dreams and my déjà vu moments being pieces of a bigger puzzle. Maybe they're more than just dreams or wow-that-was-strange moments. Maybe they're memories of a past life I shared with Nathan in this very town over one hundred years ago. I know better than anyone else that sometimes the unexplained doesn't have a simple or scientific answer. Sometimes we need to accept things on faith and instinct alone. My instinct says Nathan's dreams are more than just dreams. Am I brave enough to explore our connection to the past and the impact it may have on our present?

Chapter
5

Back on campus, we enter through the double wood doors and enter into the rotunda—the site of the accident—with its intricate chandelier hanging overhead and marble tiled floor and grand staircase rising from it like a spiral wave. There are little cherubs and flowers carved on the railings, leftover relics from the Victorian era when Charles Haunting was way into the go-big-or-go-home show of wealth for his decorating choices for the hotel. He meant to impress, and, no matter how many times I walk through these doors, the beauty still takes my breath away.

"Those guys look like they're straight out of a horror movie." Jay motions at a row of cherubs on the wooden railing. "I feel like they'll turn their heads and blink at me any second."

"The tourists think they're charming," I say.

"Why do you have tourists on campus?" Nathan asks. He winces and grabs at his bruised ribs as we climb the stairs. I slow down so he doesn't have to overexert himself so soon after the accident.

"The building is a historical landmark. They come to take pictures. When this was a hotel, they used to hold balls here." I motion at all the opulence around us. "The musicians played from the second floor—that leads to the dorms now—and the dining hall is just up the stairs, before you make the turn for the dorms, so the kitchen staff could bring refreshments to the guests. Now, the rotunda is kind of like the entryway to the school. The centerpiece. The first thing you see when you walk up the main steps."

Nathan glances into the dining hall as we pass but doesn't seem to be seeing it. He follows as I lead the way up another short flight of stairs to the second floor of the rotunda that holds the former orchestra pit and the entrance to the first floor of hotel-rooms-turned-dorm-rooms. Jay gets the job of carrying Nathan's plastic bag from the hospital full of his meager possessions. I didn't mean to go into tour guide mode, but it helps calm me down and dissipates most of the awkwardness I feel being with both Jay and Nathan. Whether it makes that nervous awkwardness go away, I don't know, but it pushes it to the side for a while.

"All the dorm rooms are unique since they used to be hotel rooms." I continue like the good little campus tour guide I can be in a pinch. "Girls and guys are on alternating floors. The main floor that the stairs lead from is just classrooms and storage and stuff. This is a girl's floor. Second dorm floor—your floor, if you accept Dad's admission and financial aid package—is a guy's floor, and then third dorm floor—my floor—is girls."

"I have nowhere else to go," Nathan says. It's not the most enthusiastic acceptance, but it will be good enough for Dad.

"They allow inter-dorm visitation until 7 p.m. After that, everyone has to go back to wherever they came from." I continue in my campus-tour-guide voice. "Dad doesn't mess around with dorm room infractions. If you're caught, you're in trouble, big-time."

"Guess I'll just have to work on not getting caught." Nathan raises both eyebrows and smiles when I look at him. Jay snickers, which doesn't help.

"Dude, don't even try it," Jay says. "Just enjoy your free ride and milk the fame from the accident as long as you can. Being famous on campus, being famous in this whole town, goes a long way. Trust me, I know."

Nathan halts. I reach out a hand, thinking his ribs hurt him, but he waves my concern away. He pinches his nose with his thumb and index finger, which is what I do when I get one of my vertigo déjà vu moments. Is it happening to him now too?

"Nathan?" My voice comes out thin and reedy, betraying my fear. Why can't I play it cool like Jay? I'm so good at hiding my emotions. Why can't I hide them with Nathan?

"I just need a sec." Nathan sways in place. I hold my breath, counting in my head. *One, two, three, four, five.* At six, he opens his eyes and stands up straight. "Well, that was weird."

I'm afraid to ask, but I do it anyway. "What happened?"

"I saw this hallway, but the lights were gas and not electric. I was running, but I'm not sure why." Nathan rubs his eyes again before shaking his head. "I don't know if I was running away from something or—"

"To someone." I clamp both hands over my mouth. "I'm sorry. I don't know why I said that."

Nathan gives me an I-know-why-you-said-that look. I just shake my head and mouth, "Don't." Jay, being Jay, stays oblivious to what's going on right in front of him regarding me. Or at least I think he's oblivious. Sometimes I think Jay notices everything and just pretends to notice nothing. Instead of warning Nathan to back off or saying any other typical confrontational macho doublespeak, Jay unlocks his dorm room—now Nathan's dorm too—and pushes the door open.

"Just so you know, Vale, this roomie thing was not my idea," he says. "You can thank Meredith's dad for that. *My* dad made sure I made it three and a half years here without a roommate. Then spring semester of my senior year, Mer's dad sticks you in here with me. Don't expect me to be happy about it."

Jay never talks about his dad or why he's perfectly happy to live on campus when his parents are less than ten minutes away. I've managed to put the puzzle pieces together over the years about what he only calls a "darkness" at home, but I don't ask for details. I only hope Jay knows I'll listen when—or if—he's ready to talk.

I shake the bad feeling away that I have about Jay's dad before I follow the boys into the room. Nathan looks around. Jay's built a shrine to himself with ski trophies, ribbons, and framed newspaper articles that decorate every available space. I've been in here what feels like a million times, but it always catches me a little off guard. I can only imagine how Nathan feels. Boom. In case you didn't feel inferior already, you're in the presence of a local sports legend.

"So, you're the same Jay Jameson who's all over the news?" Nathan asks. "The one who turned down going pro to finish up your senior year?"

"The one and only." Jay chucks Nathan's plastic hospital bag of stuff on the spare bed before he kicks off his shoes and sits down in the chair next to his computer desk. He's used to being a local celebrity and golden boy. Being recognized isn't anything new to him.

"If you're as serious about skiing as the papers and TV reports say, I'd have thought you'd jump at the chance to go pro," Nathan says. "Why'd you stick around?"

"I wanted to spend more time with Mer." Jay winks at me. I'm not sure if he's showing off in front of Nathan or if that wink is some guy code I fail at reading, but I do my best to ignore it. I do my best to ignore a lot of things around campus. Life is easier that way when you don't go looking for trouble or, with Nathan's dreams and my déjà vu moments, looking for answers.

"If you ask me, turning down going pro sounds like something you can hold over Meredith," Nathan says. "By giving up something so big for her, she owes you. I mean, even if you haven't said it yet, I bet you think it all the time. I bet you think, 'I gave up going pro for you.'"

Jay purses his lips, which is never a good sign—it means he's holding in his temper. He may be laid-back and oblivious most of the time, but when he's upset, his words cut sharper than a knife. "I'm not asking you, so back off."

Nathan holds up his hands in surrender but still continues to push Jay's buttons. What was Dad thinking by putting these two together in one tiny dorm room? "Meredith doesn't owe you anything just because you won trophies and she calls herself your girlfriend," Nathan says. "Why don't *you* back off."

"Drop it, both of you, please," I jump in before harsh words can turn to more. "I'm standing right here, okay? Don't act like I'm not. You two have to live together, remember? Just drop it and attempt to be civil, please."

"I'm cool. It's your boy Vale you need to be giving the pep talk to." Jay stands and heads into the bathroom. He shuts the door behind him, and we hear the shower start up a couple seconds later. Even though Jay showered after practice, he has a habit of getting a second one in later the same day. It's a superstitious thing. I don't remember when it started, but he says if he showers twice a day during ski season, he wins more meets.

"Well, your boyfriend is very confident or idiotic to leave the two of us alone together." Nathan smiles, showing he's joking.

I relax and even laugh. "Jay's all talk. Trust me. He's on a scholarship too. He wouldn't risk all that this close to graduation and going pro. He's got his reputation to uphold."

"Is that why you date the boy wonder of the ski team?" Nathan asks. "Reputation?"

"So, we're back to this?" I bite my bottom lip. "Jay helped me through a really tough time two years ago. Why I date Jay now is none of your business, Nathan."

"It is if you're with him because it's what people expect instead of what you want. Being a pawn—anyone's pawn, Meredith—is not for you. No one deserves to be put in a little box and kept as a prize."

"Is that what you think is happening to me?"

"That's what I know is happening to you."

Nathan takes a step toward me as I take a step back. It's like a delicate dance—one step forward, one step back until I'm pressed up against the door with Nathan standing toe to toe with me. I gaze into his eyes. Why didn't I ever notice they were as blue as a mountain lake on a clear day before? I fumble for the doorknob, holding onto the cool metal as if it is an anchor keeping me from doing something I'll regret.

"You're not just something pretty for the boy wonder to trot out and show off," Nathan whispers. "As I see it, the problem is you've backed yourself into a corner, you've fallen into that little box, and you don't know how to get out. You want to get out, don't you, Meredith? I can help you get out."

"I don't know." I push on the door to escape his words, his eyes; to escape everything about him that is pulling me in when I should push away. "It doesn't matter what I want."

Nathan follows me out into the empty hallway. "Of course it matters. It matters because *you* matter. You have a mind—a superb one from what I can tell in the short time I've known you—so you don't have to go along with what everyone expects of you. This isn't the 1800s. You're an independent person with independent goals. Don't be something or someone you're not just to please a handful of people who, when given the choice between you and their career, I'm sure they would pick their career."

I hear the shower water stop. Jay will be out any minute. Time is running out before I need to switch from independent-Meredith to trophy-girlfriend-Meredith. "We all make choices. Don't pick apart mine, Nate."

"Nathan," he corrects.

I blink as if waking from a dream. "What was that?"

"Nathan," he repeats. "My name is Nathan. You called me Nate. Again."

Before I have time to answer— or better yet, deny—the name slip-up, Jay emerges from the bathroom. He sticks his head out into the hallway when he can't find us inside.

"What are you doing out there?" he asks.

"Just, uh, talking." Judging by Jay's pursed lips, he believes me about as much as I believe myself, which is not at all.

"Well, get inside. Hanging out in the hall is just weird."

Nathan and I follow orders like someone caught us doing what we might have been doing if Jay hadn't turned off the shower at the exact moment he did. Not that I'm into cheating, nor have I ever considered it, but my body doesn't seem to want to listen to my brain since Nathan showed up in my life. Jay stoops to check his hair in the mirror above the dresser. Maybe what I always took for indifference or obliviousness in Jay is confidence with a dose of possessiveness simmering just below the surface. I've never given him a reason to distrust me, but this isn't the first time I've seen flashes of his temper.

"Do you play any sports, Vale?" Jay asks Nathan.

"Not really," he says. "I've skied before but never on a team."

Jay seems more interested in this news. He turns to survey Nathan as if trying to decide if he could keep up on the slopes or not. "We need alternates for the ski team. Tryouts are next week after classes. I had the newbs hang posters around campus if you need the where and when."

"Because it's too hard to tell me yourself, you want me to look for a poster?"

"Geez, lazy much?" Jay moves his history and math book on his desk and finds a spare flyer underneath. He holds it out to Nathan. "Here. And you call *me* entitled."

"Jay. Behave," I warn.

"What are you talking about, Mer? I always behave." Jay wanders over and wraps his arms around my waist from behind before leaning around to plant a kiss half on my mouth, half on my cheek. Instead of relaxing into his arms, I stiffen. It feels like he's trying to remind Nathan of what is his—me. I squirm in his grasp, but it just makes Jay tighten his arms instead of letting me go.

"Let go, Jay, I'm not your property!" The words are out before I realize it's my voice saying them. I pry his fingers apart and escape to stand by the still-open door. "I don't need you acting all macho sexist caveman over me. It's embarrassing."

"Macho sexist caveman?" Jay rolls his eyes. "Please, Mer, if I acted all macho sexist caveman over you, you'd know. Since when does being happy to see my girlfriend and wanting to stand close to her make me a macho sexist caveman?"

"You know I'm not into PDA. It makes me uncomfortable."

He crosses his arms over his chest. He's heard what he considers a lot of excuses from me over the last two years with public and non-public displays of affection. "A lot of things make you uncomfortable, Mer."

"Why don't you back off, Jameson?" Nathan comes to my rescue. "She said she's uncomfortable with how you were acting, end of story. That's all she should need to tell you. Meredith doesn't owe you an explanation, and you shouldn't expect one from her. Like she said, she's not your property, so back off."

"Oh, this will be a real fun semester sharing a room with you," Jay sneers. "Any more pearls of wisdom you'd like to share since you seem to think you know so much about me and my relationship, newbie?"

"Just treat her right."

"And if I don't?" he challenges.

"Then don't be surprised if someone else steals her out from under your macho sexist caveman nose."

"Someone like you?" Jay smirks. I can't tell if he's amused or bored. Nathan, to his credit, continues to stand up for himself.

"Yeah, someone like me."

"Are you both through?" I do my best to make my voice icy, so they get the point that I'm not happy with their behavior. "If you've worked the snippy fighting out of your systems, can you two at least *try* to get along? I'd add 'for me,' but that would probably start World War III."

"Hey, I can be mature if the newbie can." Jay sticks out his hand to shake on it. "We only have to live together; we don't have to like each other."

"I think that's the most intelligent thing you've said since we met." Nathan reaches out to accept Jay's offered hand. "We don't have to like each other; we only have to live together."

Chapter 7

Once I'm back inside my dorm, I turn my school clothes into a pile of khaki and green on the floor and change into sweatpants and a t-shirt. I crawl into bed and lie staring at the ceiling. My mind replays the events of the last two days. Nathan's accident, the weirdness in the rotunda, the even weirder-ness that Nathan and I connected so much while Nathan was in the hospital, and the heavy tension in Jay's room.

I don't know what it is, but ever since I met Nathan, I feel more confident in sticking up for myself and voicing my opinion. Two days won't erase a lifetime of patterns, but I'll start with baby steps. Jay and I have a pattern I feel stuck in. He suggests something, I agree, he's happy, I'm not unhappy, but I'm not happy either. I don't know how to make myself happy all the time. I feel Nathan has suggestions, if I'm willing to listen.

It might be just me, but Nathan seemed more upset about me leaving than Jay did. Before leaving their dorm, I stood around waiting for Jay or even Nathan to override my insistence I needed to study for my English Lit test. Normally, I say something, people ignore it. That is my life. When neither did, I left, but waited outside the door expecting to hear some horrific fight between them. Or one (or both) of the boys to come after me. All was quiet and the door stayed shut. I waited a minute or two before heading off down the hall to the staircase that leads to my room on the third floor.

And now I'm lying on my bed, not studying, and thinking of Nathan instead of my boyfriend. Two days. It's not much time to know someone. I feel like I know Nathan better in two days than I know Jay after two years. Nathan and I click. I can't think of another way to describe it. It doesn't feel like two days. It feels like *forever*.

All of Nathan's talk of trusting fate might be a defense mechanism, but maybe there's something more to it. He *was* super perceptive with how things run in my life. I'm always the good daughter, the good girlfriend, but all that hides an unhappy girl under the perfect exterior. How could Nathan know that if he didn't know me on some deep-down spiritual soul level? Maybe there is something to his talk of dreams and lessons learned (or not learned) from the past. Maybe I shouldn't brush it aside so easily and listen—really listen—and learn.

"Do I really want to go poking around the past if it's going to affect the present?" I ask out loud to reassure myself that I'm here in the present and not stuck on the past. "I'm Meredith, not Mercy."

Abigail suddenly appears beside my bed. I sit up, startled. No matter how many times I've seen my ghost maid appear and disappear, I always jolt at the sight of someone materializing out of thin air.

"Abigail! Can't you warn me before you do that?"

"Sorry." She shimmers slightly. "What has Nathan told you? Does he remember?"

"Remember what?" I ask.

She opens her mouth, hesitates, then shakes her head. "I've said too much already. What happened to Mercy and Nate is not my story to tell."

That gets my attention. I swing my legs over the side of my bed and lean as far toward her as I can. I mean it to be a come-on-spill-the-details, girl-talk sort of move, but Abigail was raised in the late 1800s. To her, it's probably the rich-girl-is-going-to-get-me-in-trouble-if-I-talk move. "Abigail, what do you know?"

"I'm sorry. I've said too much already. I've said too much."

"Nathan says the reason we've been slipping up and calling each other Nate and Mercy since we met is because we *were* Nate and Mercy back when the school was a hotel," I say. "Do you think that's true?"

"I think he could be on to something, miss," Abigail says. "It's a very likely reason. Memories stick with us—especially when there is unfinished business in our souls."

"You were alive then, weren't you?" I press.

"I was, miss."

"Did you know Nate and Mercy?"

Abigail flickers, which means her emotions are running high. "I'd rather not say. I'm not sure if it's proper or not to give you too much information about your past."

"It's a simple question, Abigail. You either knew them or you didn't."

"I'd rather not say," she repeats.

Something she said catches in my brain. "Wait, did you say *my* past? Don't you mean Mercy's?"

Abigail turns almost translucent in her fear. "Please, please don't make me say more."

"Fine." I flop back onto my bed. "But if you could tell me, you would, right?"

"Oh, yes, miss, I'd do anything for you." Abigail wrings her hands in front of her. "I just don't know the rules, that's all. I can ask someone, if you like. There're rules about these things you know, even in the afterlife."

"I'm sorry if I made you uncomfortable."

The tension leaves Abigail's spirit. She even smiles at me. "It's not a problem, miss. If our places were reversed, I would ask questions too."

I pick up my English text book to reread the poems we're being tested on tomorrow. I don't mean for it to be a signal of "get out of my room," but Abigail takes it as that. She's just too polite to say it.

"Will you be needing anything else tonight, miss?"

"No, thank you, Abigail, and please just call me Meredith. I can't get used to the whole 'miss' thing."

Abigail bows, which is even weirder, before disappearing.

What did she mean before by "my past" instead of "Mercy's past?" Did it mean the dream is more than I thought it was? Could Mercy and I be the same person—the same soul? I haven't read much about reincarnation and past lives, but I know enough to keep quiet about that too. Potential past lives. Ghosts at school. The quieter I am about those, the better.

I shake my head. It is all *too much*. I need a distraction. I grab my English Lit textbook and study until I'm positive I will dream about these poems. Instead, when I close my eyes, I dream I'm dancing under the lights of the dining hall, but it's not the dining hall; it's the ballroom, and I'm not me, I'm Mercy. I'm wearing a blue dress, and I twirl and twirl until I'm dizzy. Someone—a waiter in a white tuxedo jacket and black pants who I know is Nate—hands me a glass of champagne. He gives me a wink and a smile and mouths, "Later, our spot." I wink back before downing the entire glass of champagne in one gulp. I'm happy, I'm young, but, most of all, I'm in love. The part of me that knows I'm dreaming, the part that knows I'm not twirling around the ballroom, tries to pick up on all the intricate little clues and relationship patterns I'm supposed to be learning from so I don't repeat the mistakes of the past in the present, but I can't. Everything is whirling by so fast. I know I'm missing something. But what is it?

He's as inviting as sunshine.

The words slip through my mind like they're my own thoughts in that moment right between wake and sleep the next morning. It's like a whisper pulling me into another time and place. I roll over and check the red illuminated numbers on my alarm clock. 2 a.m. Abigail once said that, back in her day, they knew 2 a.m. as the "witching hour"—the time when the veil between our world and the afterlife was the thinnest. Charles Haunting himself was big into the occult and held séances in the rotunda at 2 a.m., hoping to make a stronger connection to the spirit realm. Maybe that's another reason the ghosts that linger have such a hard time moving on. There were too many people messing around with forces they shouldn't have been. Despite Charles Haunting founding the town and turning it into a tourist trap that hasn't let up even today, from what I've learned about the real man from Abigail versus what I heard in the legends, I don't like him very much. He ruled the hotel with an iron fist. That fear still reverberates long after everyone has been dead and buried.

I flop onto my back and watch my ceiling fan glide around and around. For a hot second, I think about sneaking down to the second floor and knocking on Jay and Nathan's dorm room, but even I don't know which boy I'd be asking for or which one I'd want to answer the door. That's a problem. That's a big problem. Instead of dealing with my suddenly complicated love life, I force myself to recall the details of my dream. It wasn't the first time I've dreamed of being Mercy. They started after Mom died. This is the first time I feel like I might be seeing the same thing as Nathan, but from a different perspective. When we hung out in the hospital, Nathan talked a lot about dreaming of his past as Nate. I think my past as Mercy is where the "he's as inviting as sunshine" thought comes from. I've never thought anyone looked as inviting as sunshine. Sunshine is hot and burns and isn't as magical as it's cracked up to be. Sunshine means no ski season, and no ski season means Jay needs something else to focus most of his attention on. When you live in a state that claims three hundred days of sunshine a year, you'd think sunshine would be inviting, but not to me. Not now. Sunshine means confinement, possession, being put in my box and being told to stay there. It's not inviting. Not in the least bit. That's why it can't be me thinking the thought. It has to be her. It has to be Mercy.

Everything I see in the dreams plays out like a first-person video game from Mercy's point of view. I can't tell any "normal" details about her like what her clothes look like or what color her hair is, but I know she sneaks off from the fancy-pants hotel her father runs—*this* fancy-pants hotel—every afternoon to meet *him*.

Nate.

I can tell you everything about him. He's not that tall, he's thin, and he has reddish-brown hair and freckles across his nose. I could sketch him a thousand times over if my art skills were any good. It's like she memorized every detail about him in case something happened. Nate's Irish but tries to hide the accent. Maybe they were still being discriminated against back then, and he didn't want to be taken for just another "mick" looking for work. His smile could light up a room, and his laugh is so contagious that sometimes, even now, I wake up from laughing out loud right along with him. Every night, Mercy and Nate show me what it's like to be in love with someone. I can pick up on those blatant clues enough to know that how Mercy feels about Nate is not how I feel about Jay. With Jay, it feels like I'm just marking time. I'm not even sure what I'm waiting for. Maybe I'm waiting for him to graduate as an excuse to drift apart.

I don't even know anymore.

Staying together is easier than breaking up. It's easier to be the good girl and stay in my box than try to break free. So what if I don't have a big epic love like Nate and Mercy? Big deal. Not everyone feels that way. That doesn't mean their relationship isn't valid; it just means it's different. A voice—maybe my conscience or guilt over thinking about Nathan when I have a respectable boyfriend already —whispers in my mind, *do you feel that way about Nathan?*

"How should I know?" I answer out loud. "I barely know the guy."

But I want to get to know him, a voice in my head whispers.

Now I recognize it. It's my heart betraying my head once again.

I wouldn't say Nathan is waiting for me outside of Professor Lewis's Colorado History class, but he's hovering near the door. What's more, he's looking mighty good in clothes dressier than most wear to an 8 a.m. class—rolling out of bed and grabbing the first thing that your hands find in your dresser seems to be the normal dress code around here. The second the words "looks good" slip through my mind, I beat myself up for it. Jay's in this class too. He was short a history credit and took Colorado History 101 because he thought it was a fluff class, plus I was in it. Jay seemed to schedule a lot of his classes because I was in them. Most people thought the habit was charming. I thought it was possessive. But I'm comfortable with Jay, aren't I? *Yes.* He's safe. There's something to be said for picking the safe path or person. There are fewer surprises that way.

"Need help with figuring your schedule out?" I say as I stop in front of Nathan.

He grins in relief—his whole body relaxes when he notices it's me. "I think I'm in the right place, but the room numbers on the schedule are confusing." He holds out his schedule to show me. "This is the second floor, right, so the room number should start with a two, but it doesn't. It says Room 325. How can Room 325 be on the second floor?"

"Because the lobby counts as the first floor," I explain. "Technically speaking, this is the third floor even though you only went up two flights of stairs. So, lobby classrooms start with a one, first floor rooms start with a two, and second floor rooms start with a three."

"Thanks. That helps."

"You're welcome."

Nathan just stands there watching me like he wants to say something more but is afraid to. Did he dream about Nate and Mercy last night too? Does he know as much about them as I do? Did he spend half the night debating whether or not to break inter-dorm visitation rules like I did? There's so much I want to say, but nothing comes out. But that doesn't mean *he* has to stay silent.

"If you want to talk to me, just talk to me, Nathan." I grab his hand and pull him down the hall and around the corner so Jay can't see us when he graces the class with his presence. "We don't have much time. Did Jay tell you he's taking Colorado History too?"

"The less Jay and I talk the better," Nathan replies.

"That's probably for the best." I look around as if expecting Jay to pop up and ruin this stolen moment between Nathan and me. Is this how Mercy felt? Is this why she ran away to meet up with Nate? Was there someone in her life who didn't understand that she needed to run away from them?

"Well, there is something I want to talk to you about," Nathan admits.

I let go of his hand once I realize I'm still holding on to it. "Go ahead. I promise not to laugh or think you're weird or anything. I'm the last person who should call someone weird. There are, well, there are *things* that go on here that you don't know about yet that make it impossible for me to call anyone weird. That's just...Well, I, uh...I'll be quiet now and let you talk. If you want to talk, that is. You don't have to talk, it's just—" I bite down hard on my lower lip to make the nervous flood of words stop. "Uh, I bet you can see why I'm a loner. Outside of Jay, the only person who even talks to me is my suite-mate Ritzi. No one else wants to hang out with the dean of admissions's daughter who happens to suffer from verbal diarrhea, among other issues."

Nathan laughs. The sound is natural and soothing. It makes me think suddenly of Nate standing next to the lake with the sun and wind catching his tawny hair and making it glow. "You're funny," he says and seems to mean it. "I wanted to talk to you about what I said in the hospital. I didn't mean to scare you or come across all stalker-esque with that talk about dreams and knowing you better than you know yourself. I usually take a girl out for coffee or something first before springing the whole possible-soulmate connection on them. Sorry, I got ahead of myself there. Blame it on the concussion. So, what do you say? Coffee sometime soon?"

I smile, feeling more relaxed around Nathan after days than I feel after years around Jay. "I prefer food over coffee and, the way you talk, it makes it sound like the possible-soulmate thing is your standard pickup line."

"Only with short blonde girls with self-diagnosed cases of verbal diarrhea who also happen to be the dean of admissions's daughter."

"You do remember that I have a boyfriend, right?" I remind him, though I keep my tone playful and light.

Nathan grins. "Yeah, I remember, but that doesn't mean I like it or think he's the right guy for you. So, is that a yes for the coffee?"

I open my mouth to come back with something cool and witty sounding, but the warning bell rings and puts an end to the small fraction of flirting we're doing. "One-minute warning. Professor Lewis hates when people come to class late." I grab Nathan's hand again and pull him back down the hall and inside the classroom before I realize that maybe I don't want to be touching him—even just somewhere normal like his hand. He doesn't need fuel for his possible soulmate theory, and I don't need to be reminded, thanks to the electric tingling in my hand when Nathan and I touch, of Jay's and my relationship shortcomings. *Jay is safe*, I remind myself. *Stick with safe.*

I maneuver my way down the rows of desks to sit in my usual seat behind Ritzi. If I told anyone besides Nathan about the "I see dead people" stuff, it would be her. She's got an earthy, chill vibe that makes me want to confide in her. I don't because trust is hard for me, but Ritzi would be high on my list of confidantes.

Ritzi turns in her chair when she notices me sit down while Nathan finds a seat in the row next to me. "What do you think of the new do?" She motions to her dyed hair. Half of it is bright pink, the other half is bright purple, the colors separated straight down the middle part.

I smile. "I love it. Only you could pull something like that off, Ritzi." While I'm thinking, I point at Nathan. "This is Nathan. He's the new transfer student."

"Hey, there. Your reputation proceeds you." Her eyes light up in a way I don't like once they talk, but I can't say anything about it because Jay saunters in at the last possible second as the final bell is tolling.

Professor Lewis, as is his usual thing, starts class the second the late bell rings. "You're late, Mr. Jameson."

"No, I'm not, Professor Lewis." Jay throws the professor one of his good-natured, golden-boy lopsided grins, expecting it to fix everything. "The bell is still going. I'm right on time." He slides into his usual seat next to me and gives me a wink as if I'm in on his troll-the-teacher routine, which I definitely am not.

Professor Lewis's lips thin into a tiny line. I can tell he's just itchy to tell Jay off, but no one tells Jay off—especially if they expect my dad to decide to give them tenure or not. "Good morning, people. I'd like to start our new unit off with a group project on Haunting's history. Since some of you are not from our lovely state, this will be a great way to learn about your current home, and it gives me a break from lecturing day in and day out since each group will present in front of the class on what they've discovered."

"How many people count as a group?" Jay asks.

"In this instance, a group means three," Professor Lewis says. "And I mean three people total, Mr. Jameson, not three classmates plus you."

"Picked or assigned?" Jay fires off another all-important question. I know where he's going with this. If we get to pick our own group, he'll pick me, whether or not I want to be in his group. It's a given we'll be together. All to make sure his good girl keeps being good. I don't know where that leaves Nathan, let alone Ritzi, but those are the two other people I'd want in my group of three if we got to pick our groups.

"Assigned," Professor Lewis says. "I don't have time for petty school politics or popularity contests. You'll work with who I say you work with, end of discussion."

"But—" Jay starts, only to be cut off by Professor Lewis.

"What part of 'end of discussion' don't you understand, Mr. Jameson?"

"I'll let you know once I hear the group assignments, Professor."

Professor Lewis looks down his class roster and calls out names at random. I don't realize I'm holding my breath till I let it out in a big sigh of relief when he calls "Group number three: Nathan Vale, Meredith Monroe, Ritzi Carmichael." Jay ends up with Sally Jenkins and Roberto Tally. Not a bad group by any stretch of the imagination, but not the one he was expecting. His hand shoots up.

"Do you have a problem, Mr. Jameson?"

I got to give Professor Lewis credit for keeping his voice so level and even.

"I need to switch groups," Jay says.

"Sorry, not going to happen," Professor Lewis says. "All group assignments are final."

"Then I need you to bend the rules and make a group of four. I need to be in Meredith's group." He leans forward in his desk; his eyes, face, expression, and body language drip intensity. I squirm in my seat. I've rarely seen him this intense, and never over me. Is the thought of being apart from me that upsetting? This is a different side of Jay. A side I'm not sure I like.

"Sorry, Mr. Jameson, the rules still hold. Now, time to get into your new groups, people. It's assignment time." Professor Lewis motions for us to push our desks together, and we do. I can tell by their bright expressions that Ritzi and Nathan are excited about the group assignment. Jay gives me a dramatic, longing look before he drags himself across the room to sit with Sally and Roberto.

"Each group will have three weeks to prepare their presentation," Professor Lewis continues. "I expect extensive research notes and a paper to go along with your in-class presentations. All the directions are on the papers I'm passing out now." Professor Lewis drops assignment packets on each of the desk clusters. "Make the past come to life, people. That's a requirement, not a request."

I glance down at our assignment. I have that same whooshing vertigo feeling, but, this time, I feel like I'm going to throw up. I cover my mouth and notice my hand is shaking. I'm not the only one who notices.

"Meredith?" Nathan puts his hand over mine. He means it to be comforting, but it only makes me shake more. "What it is? What's wrong?"

I jab an unsteady finger at our paper. "1880s Haunting and the occult. Do you know what this means?"

"What? A lot of rich, Victorian people believed in the supernatural." Ritzi shrugs. "It was way trendy back then to do séances and take spirit photographs and a million other things. This will be a piece of cake to research. Don't worry, we got this in the bag, Meredith."

I shake my head. "No, you don't understand. It also means we have to go to graveyards and the psychic shops in town." I swallow hard to keep the bile down. "I *hate* those places. They're too busy."

Nathan frowns as if he can tell I'm not telling the whole truth. "Busy how?"

I rub my arms as a sudden chill overtakes me. It feels as if someone ran their ghostly fingers down my back. "There's just too much history in this town. It's spooky. I want no part of the occult." I didn't add that despite having a ghost friend and being able to see and talk to anyone on the other side, it doesn't mean I want to hang around a graveyard. Psychic mediums in a graveyard is like an all-you-can-eat buffet for ghosts. They all rush to you begging for help or to deliver messages to still-living relatives. I want to help. I want them to be at peace. But there's *just too many of them*. It's overwhelming. There's only one of me and hundreds of ghosts. Everywhere I look I see them. I ignore them as best I can, which is not very helpful of me, but I need to do it. I need to ignore my psychic abilities as much as possible or risk losing my sanity. It's a choice. I'm not happy with it, but it's the choice I needed to make for me.

"I think we lucked out project-wise," Ritzi says, not noticing my long silence. "I don't know about you, but I've been into the metaphysical stuff for a while—it's what first brought me to Haunting Academy—and there's so much source material to draw from. We could focus on tons of topics. Charles Haunting's obsession with the afterlife, whether the ghost stories about the town are true or not, if they have their roots in the 1800s, occult symbolism in the hotel building. I think Professor Lewis did us a favor by giving us this topic."

"I'm game," Nathan agrees. "You in, Meredith?"

I shake my head. It feels heavy and kind of hazy, like I have a fever I can't shake. "No, Nate, you don't understand. I can't do it. I can't go back there."

"Nathan." He corrects before I realize I've slipped up again. He puts a hand on either side of my face and leans in close so I can see the bright blue of his eyes. "Stick with me here in the present, okay, Meredith? You don't have to go back. You're right here, right now. You don't have to go back. Stick with me, okay?"

I close my eyes and take deep, steadying breaths to rein in my thoughts and emotions that threaten to scatter and pull me back to the past. I don't need that now. As Nathan said, I can control this. I don't need to go back there. I focus on the pressure of his hands on my cheeks. I let the comfort and safety I feel around Nathan seep into me and wash away the fear. I don't need to go back there. Just because I now dream of those people from the past doesn't mean I now need to deal with them while I'm awake. I open my eyes.

"You okay?" Nathan asks.

"Do you think we can switch with someone for a new topic?"

"I like this one," he says. "Besides, it might do good to face your fears. Local graveyards and psychics can't be as bad as you think, right?"

I laugh, but it's far from a happy sound. "Wanna bet?"

Chapter 10

We've barely cleared the door after class when Jay corners Nathan in the hall. I want to run away so I don't have to face whatever will happen next, but my feet won't cooperate. I stand rooted in place, watching as if it's all happening to someone else.

"Hey, Vale, switch groups with me."

Nathan swings around to face Jay. "Not on your life, Jameson. Professor Lewis said assigned, so I'm sticking with what he assigned. You may be used to ordering people around and getting what you want because you win a bunch of trophies, but I'm new here, and I will play by the rules."

"But I'm always with Mer."

"Maybe that's the problem." Nathan's mouth turns up in a half-smirk. "What's wrong? Are you so insecure that you can't spend three weeks working on a research project away from your girlfriend? She's still in class, Jameson, just not in your group."

"You can trust me." The words are out before I realize I ever intended to speak up. "I've never given you reason not to, have I?"

Jay looks like he's considering the idea. "I guess you're right." He walks over and kisses the center of my forehead, then both of his hands wrap around my wrists. He taps the Claddagh ring on my right hand with one long finger. "Just remember who gave you that and what it means, okay?"

The world, or at least my world, tips, and I'm lost in the past. I see the same scene that replays over and over, whether I'm awake or asleep, with the ballroom and dancing. This time, a blond man in a fancy, old-fashioned tuxedo steps forward and holds out his hand to me or—more accurately—to Mercy. Mercy takes his hand and allows herself to be led out onto the dance floor where they twirl under the lights until everything becomes a blur of colors and laughter. At the end of the dance, the blond man casually pulls out a ring box as if a girl gets pricey jewelry at the end of every dance. It's not a Claddagh ring, but the meaning is the same: You belong to me.

I gasp as I pull myself out of the memory. Jay and Nathan come into focus. "I-I'm sorry," I say. "I have to go. I-I can't do this. I just can't."

I don't know where I'm going, but my feet take me to the staircase, down two flights of stairs, across the quad, and back to the main dorm building. I hear Nathan calling my name, but I put my head down and keep walking. I stop in front of what I call my safe zone—-the dark little alcove hidden under the rotunda stairs that used to lead to a secret passage or something when the school was still a hotel. I tuck myself inside and close my eyes to hide from the memories and all the amped-up weirdness of the last few days. It's not like my life was normal before, but it's gone into overdrive since Nathan's arrival.

"Meredith?" I crack open an eye as Nathan sticks his head into my hiding spot. "You okay?"

"I can't go back there, Nate. I can't. Please don't make me."

"It's Nathan. Stay with me here, okay, Meredith?" He squeezes in next to me, though we both have to sit with our legs tucked up to our chests. Nathan waits for my breathing to stop being all ragged and return to normal before saying, "Tell me what scares you about digging around in the town's past."

"Everything."

"You got to be more specific than that." He bumps his shoulder against mine. It's a friendly we're-in-this-together gesture.

"I should tell you about the school first," I say.

"What about it?" Nathan asks. "It used to be a hotel. Your dad runs the place. He gave me a big scholarship. You're here, which means I want to be here. What's more to know?"

"It's full of ghosts," I confess. "If you stick around long enough, you'll find out what I mean. The elevator does its own thing, and there's always someone watching you, touching your shoulder, moving your stuff. I don't know why I'm even telling you this, or if you'll even believe me, but I needed to tell someone."

"So, you picked me?"

I shrug. "I can't quite explain why, but I'll try. You talk about some connection, and I feel it too. There's something there, even if I deny it or run away from it. I guess what it comes down to is trusting you. I trust you, Nathan. I'm not used to trusting anyone with my secrets, so that's why I picked you to talk to about the weird stuff that goes on at school."

He bows as much as he can while huddled up on a bench. "I'm flattered and honored. Thank you, Meredith. Now define 'weird stuff.'"

"Things move around or go missing. Music plays in the middle of the night. Doors open and close. Nothing bad has ever happened to anyone on campus until your accident, but everything is so unsettled. There's too much history here, especially in this building. There's a restlessness that I can feel almost as if it's a living, breathing thing. I see them. I see them all, and they need help. They need help, and I can't save them. I'm just one person. It's overwhelming. Dad turned a haunted hotel into a haunted school, and nobody knows but me."

Nathan puts a hand on my knee for added comfort. "Is that why you stick to being a loner? Because you're afraid everyone will think you're just the freaky 'I see dead people' daughter of the dean of admissions?"

I swipe a hand under my damp eyes. "Well, aren't I a freak? At least, that's what everyone used to think when I still talked about it. I learned to keep quiet really quick and just deal alone, silent and afraid. The school is full of ghosts, but the town is worse. There's too much—too much—for anyone to get any peace here." I shake my head, trying to clear the memory of the last time I stepped foot near a graveyard. "Trust me, you don't even want to know what it's like for me to go anywhere near a cemetery."

"I believe you, but I still think keeping our project topic and facing your fears is the only way for you to heal," Nathan says. "Maybe you're unsettled just like the town. Maybe facing your fears is the only way to be at peace."

I smile, feeling a little more relaxed already. "Thanks. I never thought of it like that before."

Nathan bumps my shoulder in that friendly we're-a-team way of his again. "No problem." He takes a deep breath before adding, "The real reason I applied to Haunting Academy is not because I wanted to list a fancy, well-known school on my résumé, but because I've known about Nate and Mercy since I first had dreams about them three years ago. I've been trying to get back here, not run away."

"Trying to get back here?" The pressure of his hand on my knee is comforting and familiar and makes me *want* to talk about the past instead of hiding all reference to it away like I normally do. "Why would you want to do that?"

"Because I knew you would wait," he says. "I just had to get back here first."

I scoot a little closer and lean my head against Nathan's shoulder. He moves his hand from my knee to my waist and draws me closer. It's a relief to have this be *our* dream and *our* secret instead of just mine and mine alone to deal with.

"What are the dreams like for you?" I ask.

"Nate's on the beach waiting for Mercy," he begins. "She looks a lot like you, actually. Tiny. Blonde. An amazing smile. I think I would recognize you anywhere, Meredith, and I don't just mean the physical you. I mean everything about you. Your very essence. It calls to me, pulls me across the years and miles and lifetimes. I hope I'm not scaring you. I know I can be pretty intense sometimes. Nate probably could be too. That's probably a lesson I need to learn this time around. 'Don't scare the ladies with coming on too strong.'" He laughs to cover his nervousness. "Uh, *am* I scaring you with this kind of talk?"

Is he scaring me? If it were anyone but Nathan, I'd be looking for the nearest security guard, but *because* it's Nathan, I feel a sense of peace and complete acceptance. I can't explain it any more than I can explain the weird stuff that goes on at school. He's here. Maybe I've been waiting for him. Maybe we're meant to meet.

"Um, you can answer any time, you know," Nathan reminds me.

"It should scare me," I admit. "Everything rational in me says I should tase you and run while I can, but everything irrational in me says you're right. I think I was waiting too, Nathan. I just didn't know for what."

"Or who," he adds.

"If we do this Colorado History project about Haunting and the occult, we will face the past." I squeeze my eyes shut and try to keep the feeling of dread at bay. I try to tell myself that with Nathan by my side, I can face anything—just like Mercy could face anything as long as Nate was with her. "I think something happened to them, Nathan. Something bad." I take a deep breath and ask him something I didn't know I wanted to until the words fall out: "Do you want to find out what?"

Nathan nods. It's like he was just waiting for me to ask. Like he wants it to be my choice instead of his. "Yes. It's the only way to be free of the dreams and make peace with the past."

"What dream?" Jay's voice fills the space of my hiding spot. Nathan and I only have a few precious seconds to untangle ourselves and look all innocent and "just friends" before his body fills the space where his words are still echoing.

"I, uh, have this dream," I begin as Nathan and I scramble out of my safe zone to stand with Jay at the bottom of the breezeway stairs. "Wait. Make that plural. I've, uh, *had* these dreams off and on since I was twelve. I'm sure I've talked about it with you at some point."

"We met when you were twelve." Jay frowns. I can't quite tell what memory he's drudging up. "That's when my family moved to Haunting." He shakes his head before shrugging off whatever sadness the move and that time held. "You should remember that."

Has it been that long since Jay moved to Haunting? My mind goes blank as I try to pull up memories of my pre–car accident life, especially of a twelve-year-old me and fourteen-year-old Jay, but I manage to slowly pull up the images. I remember when Dad introduced Jay as "a young man you should associate with." Keeping up appearances has always been one of the most important things, if not *the* most important thing, to Dad. Jay was confident, handsome, and already a rising star on the ski slopes. His family wasted no time becoming society darlings in Haunting by throwing charity events left and right that soon turned into positions in local government. Jay may attend Haunting Academy on a ski scholarship, but that's just a formality. His family is loaded, which is just how Dad likes potential in-laws to be. That "do what I deem socially acceptable, not what you want" attitude helped push me to say yes when Jay first asked me out when I turned fourteen and Dad allowed me to date. Before I knew it, Jay and I were a couple, and I haven't been able to tell anyone different ever since.

I'm stuck in a box of my own creation.

"I remember," I say. "Dad introduced us. He wanted you to teach me how to ski."

Jay grins at the memory. "I started you out on the bunny slope. You fell your first time down and spent the rest of the trip in the lodge with a sprained ankle."

"Hey, I never said I was graceful. Or good at skiing."

"Naw, but you sure were cute."

I smile at the memory. When did things get so complicated between us? Everything was so much simpler. I reach out a hand to Jay, eager to return—even if just for a moment—to that happier time. We laugh over that long-ago ski trip filled with sprained ankles and hot chocolates by the fireplace. In its simplest form, when no one is interfering and we can just hang out with no demands or expectations, our relationship works. It's when the jealousy, possessiveness, and insecurity come out to play that things between us get crazy.

Out of the corner of my eye, I catch Nathan frowning. He looks uncomfortable over the fact that Jay and I are sharing a moment.

"We should tell Jay about the dreams, Meredith," Nathan says.

Jay looks over at Nathan as if just realizing he's standing there for the first time. "We? What do you have to do with it?"

"Oh, everything." Nathan grins, but not in the nice way. It's in the antagonize-Jay way that makes me want to turn and walk away from both. *Boys!*

"We're having the same dreams," Nathan begins. "There's this couple named Nate and Mercy. He's not the kind of guy her dad would approve of, so they have to sneak around to see each other. Neither of us is sure how things end, but probably not great if we're both being pushed in the direction to find out. Ever since I've shown up, Meredith has been slipping up and calling me Nate. Maybe there's a connection, maybe there's not, but everything happens for a reason, and we owe it to ourselves to find out what that reason is."

"You're quick to lump Mer in with your theory." Jay turns for confirmation that this is what I want, too, that Nathan is not just putting words in my mouth. "Does this have anything to do with why you ran out of class? What are you afraid of?"

"That's just it." I close my eyes and take a deep breath. The memories of the past are trying to intrude on the present, but I push them aside. "I don't know what I'm afraid of, Jay. It has something to do with the past and that it's linked to our Colorado History project, but, beyond that, I just don't know. That's what's so confusing about the whole thing. I just don't know."

"Maybe hypnotherapy can help get to the root of the fear," Nathan suggests.

"Hypnotherapy?" Jay wrinkles his nose in disgust. "Like the guy on TV who makes people think they're their favorite TV character or propose to mailboxes? How is that supposed to help Mer?"

"No. No, hypnotherapy is different," Nathan says. "Hypnotherapists use relaxation techniques to help people quit smoking or lose weight or face whatever issues they may need to face."

"Look around, Vale." Jay sweeps an arm around the rotunda. "None of us are packing on the pounds or sneaking off behind the building for a smoke break."

"Hypnotherapists do other things," Nathan insists. "Ever heard of past-life regression therapy? There's got to be a connection between the reason we keep calling each other Nate and Mercy and the dreams. Now with this Colorado History project in the mix, it seems like everything is pushing us toward finding out what that connection may be."

"What do you think of all this, Mer?" Jay asks. "Are you buying all this new-age crap?"

I close my eyes and take several deep breaths to calm my scattered thoughts and nerves before opening my eyes. I don't want to do this, I really don't, but it may be the only way to help not only me but also the restless memories of Nate and Mercy. "Okay, I can't believe I'm suggesting this. You know I wouldn't say this if I didn't believe it could help me, Jay, but let's go to Psychic Square."

Jay snorts in derision, but Nathan looks over at me. "What's Psychic Square?"

"It's like a whole community of psychics just outside of town," I say. "Some people say it's just another tourist trap, but I think if anyone can help us, someone there can. As a bonus, we might get info we can use on our project."

"I'm in if you are," Nathan says.

"And how do you plan to get there?" Jay leans against the staircase rail before crossing his arms over his chest. "Are you forgetting that little detail? Are you going to walk? Take the bus? I'm the only one with wheels, and I don't like all this new-age mumbo jumbo you're trying to feed me. Without me, you're stuck here, and I say we're not going to Psychic Square or anywhere with the word 'psychic' in it."

"But it's for school," I protest.

"Get real." Jay kicks off from the staircase and walks over to stand in front of me. His entire focus is on me. He's already become a master of ignoring Nathan. "Do you expect me to believe that? You want to work on this project as much as I do. The past is in the past for a reason. Leave it alone."

"Even if it affects the present?"

"Especially if it affects the present." Jay looks over his shoulder as if he expects someone to interrupt us. I suck in my breath as I realize he's nervous. Jay, Mr. Confident, is nervous. But of what?

I step toe to toe with Jay and wrap one arm around his neck while I use the other to turn his face back to look at me. I let my palm rest against his cheek. What is he hiding? I've never seen him like this before. "I know this is out of your comfort zone. I get that. I'm sorry if I'm asking too much of you, but I think this will be good for me. Maybe it will be good for all of us."

Jay's eyes lock with mine. He lets his curtain of bravado drop just enough for me to get a glimpse of the real boy underneath. I see a scared, insecure boy playing the part of a sports hero. My heart hurts because I've never gone digging for the truth in the almost five years I've known him. I've just always assumed what was on the surface was what was underneath too. Jay's been playing a role this whole time. An image of the blond man dancing with Mercy flashes through my mind when I look at Jay. The man's face morphs into Jay's. Were they the same soul? Do we all have a role to play? Whether we're Meredith, Nathan, and Jay or Mercy, Nate, and the guy who gave Mercy an engagement ring, our roles are the same. Would finding out about our possible past-life connections help us break the patterns we're now repeating?

"Why do you want to go to Psychic Square, Meredith?" Jay asks. "Tell me the truth—and don't just say for a good grade on your history project. I'll take you wherever you want to go. I'd drive you to the ends of the earth if you asked me to."

"I want to do this because, ever since I had the dream, it always seemed like a part of me was missing," I answer. "It's like there are pieces from a puzzle missing, and I've always wanted to see the whole picture. I've always wanted to know everything my mind is trying to tell me, but I can't do it unless I have help. Going to Psychic Square might be the only way to help."

"But thinking the universe is setting up all these coincidences just so you can have a dream explained? That's a big leap of faith, Meredith. I'm more into facts and science. You know that."

Jay pulls away from me. I hold out my hand and take a step after him before pulling back. Would he even want me to go after him? I'm far from the queen of PDA. I don't want him to think any comfort I give is contrived to get what I want instead of sincere.

"We took that psych class, Jay," I remind him. "You know how powerful the subconscious is."

"Besides, nothing is random or a coincidence if you believe in fate," Nathan adds. "I think we owe it to Meredith and to ourselves, Jay, to check this thing out. If it leads nowhere, we've only wasted gas on a trip to Psychic Square, and we can laugh about it later."

I watch Jay. He's conflicted. I see he wants to help but doesn't want to come across as *wanting* to help. I think if it were just me in the mix, or even just me asking, he'd do it. But it's not just me; there's Nathan. Nathan is a big part of the equation, and he has been since the second he arrived on campus. For the first time ever, I bet Jay can see the potential cracks in our relationship. Promise ring or no promise ring, he may not hold on to me forever, and that scares the hell out of him.

"Please come with us to Psychic Square, Jay." I include him, hoping to lessen some of his fears. "Please. For me?"

"Fine." He huffs. "But you owe me."

"Just a minute!" I call when I hear a knock on my door. I'm already running late to meet Nathan and Ritzi in the school library to work on research for our Colorado History project. I don't need to be slowed down even more. To make matters worse, my text message alert beeps. I pick up my phone to check who it's from. Nathan's sent a selfie of himself surrounded by stacks of library books. He's captioned it, *wish you were here*. I send a quick *Be right there* text back before opening my door. Ritzi is standing outside in the hall.

"Hey." She looks down, scuffing her foot against the carpet. "I wasn't sure if you were already down in the library. Want to walk down together?"

"Sure." I grab my backpack and sling it over my shoulder before shutting and locking my dorm room door. At first, we walk in silence, which I'm fine with, but Ritzi is the most gregarious person I know. A silent Ritzi is just plain weird.

"What gives?" I ask as we walk through the dorms, out into the quad, and turn toward the library. "You're never this quiet. I feel like

I've slipped into an alternate dimension where I'm the talky one, and you're the loner."

Ritzi tries to smile, but it's a half-hearted effort. "I'm just...Well, maybe I can tell you...Can you keep a secret, Meredith?"

"Can I keep a secret? Please, secrets and I are BFFs." I make sure my tone is light to put her at ease. I don't have many people I feel comfortable around at school. Ritzi is one. I hope she feels the same about me.

"Okay, but don't tell him, all right?" She takes a deep breath. "I have a crush on someone, but I totally don't know how he feels about me. I keep going over and over everything in my mind, trying to look for clues and stuff, but I think I'm misreading things. I think he's nice to everyone, you know? I think he's just that sort of guy, and I'm a tool for reading too much into things."

A crush. This is standard girl stuff. After dealing with ghosts, déjà vu, and possible past-life connections, normal girl stuff is something I can definitely get behind. "So, who is the lucky guy?"

Ritzi takes another deep breath. She looks like she wants to tell me but *doesn't* want to tell me at the same time. "Nathan."

I feel like someone has punched me in the gut. All the air leaves my lungs and lights dance in front of my eyes. I'm surprised I stay on my feet. If there ever were a good time to faint, now would be it. "Nathan?" I gasp. "Nathan Vale?"

"I know, I know. I'm probably imagining the whole thing, but I thought you at least would know if he is single or not." Ritzi puts her hands up in prayer position. "Please, please tell me anything you know."

"Anything I know about what?"

"If he's single or looking or, well, anything, you know?" She gives me her puppy-dog eyes next. "Please, Meredith. I'm not desperate, but I want to get to know him better. Since the first day he came, he's been hanging with you and Jay. I thought you'd have the inside track, you know?"

"I'll, uh, see what I can find out," I promise, even though

everything in me wants to tell her to back the heck off and find someone else. I scrape both hands down my face. Ugh. What is wrong with me? It feels like I'm on some bizarre game show. *Behind door number one is your boyfriend, remember him? Behind door number two is the new kid who you shouldn't be drawn to, but you are. All this could be ruined by your one friend on campus who asked you to help facilitate getting intel on her crush. Meredith Monroe, this is your life!*

I'm ecstatic when Ritzi and I swipe our student IDs to enter the library because it means I can push relationship drama thoughts aside for a little bit and focus on school work. Nathan sees us enter and waves us over to his table.

"What subjects did you pull?" Ritzi asks. She kicks her foot like she did in the dorm hallway, which I now see as a sign of nerves.

He motions at his mountain of books. "Local history and ghost stories. Do you have any other ideas?"

"I'll find some stuff on séances."

Ritzi heads off to the stacks to search for more books. I slide into a chair across the table from Nathan. If I were a good friend, I'd try to gauge his interest in Ritzi so I'd have something to tell her later. Even though I already know what his answer will be, I try anyway.

"So, what do you think about Ritzi?" I ask.

"She seems cool enough," Nathan says. "She knows the subject, so that'll be useful on our project."

"Would you ever consider going out for coffee or anything like that?"

He looks up, his expression going from startled to confused in under ten seconds. "With Ritzi?"

"Yeah, with Ritzi," I say. "What's wrong about grabbing coffee with Ritzi?"

"Nothing's wrong with grabbing coffee with Ritzi besides the fact she's not you." Nathan reaches across the table and covers both my hands with his. "She's not you, Meredith. You're the only one I want to grab coffee or anything with. Just you. Only you."

I pull my hands away. "I can't do this, Nathan. Let's just focus on the project, okay?"

Ritzi comes back to the table with a stack of books in her arms. She sits next to Nathan. He ignores both of us for a while, flipping through books and pages, before sliding one across the table toward me.

"Hey, look at this. It will be perfect."

I glance down at the story entitled "The Mirror Room." I look up. "What's this?"

"I think it will give us an amazing angle for our project." Nathan taps the open book. "You said Charles Haunting was way into the occult. And I read that there's supposed to be secret symbolism all over the architecture of the old hotel. He's Victorian and into the occult. There's our angle."

"If it's well-documented, maybe we won't have to go to Psychic Square," I say.

"Psychic Square? When are you going to Psychic Square?" Ritzi perks up with interest. "I love it there."

"We're planning to go tomorrow," Nathan says. "We're thinking of looking for a hypnotherapist. There're some answers we need that are stuck in the past."

"We? Who is we?" Ritzi looks back and forth between Nathan and me. I bet she's hoping for an invite, though Nathan doesn't take the hint.

"Just Meredith, Jay, and me. And Jay's only coming along because we need his car." Nathan stops, his expression showing he realizes too late that he's being an ass. He backtracks as gracefully as he can. "I'd invite you along, but I don't think there's room. Jay's car is like the size of a postage stamp. Maybe next time."

Ritzi attempts a shaky smile. "Sure. Maybe next time."

I scan the short ghost story Nathan pushed my way to get out of talking about Psychic Square, looking for answers with hypnotherapy, and haunted hotels turned haunted schools. The story is about Charles Haunting's crazy second wife, Elizabeth. She stabbed him with scissors, and he locked her up in a room full of mirrors that, when the light hit them just right, wouldn't cast a reflection. At least that's how the story goes, though I doubt even Charles Haunting could get away with locking up a crazy attempted-murderer wife with no one saying anything about it. What gives me shivers is the supposed mirror room is on my dorm floor. It's locked up tight now, and Dad claims it's just a storage room, but I remember when he tried to have people stay there. Girls would hang posters and pictures on the wall, leave for class, and when they came back, everything would be on their beds in neat little stacks. They'd try everything to make the posters and pictures stick to the walls, from tape to staples to nails, and, no matter what, nothing stayed on. I remember one resident reported waking up to see a lady in an old-fashioned dress looking out the window. When the girl called to her, the lady disappeared. Even after the room was closed up, people still reported seeing a glint of glass, like sun reflecting off of mirrors, when they look up to the third-floor window from the courtyard.

The one and only time I braved walking by the mirror room, I felt an intense cold. I put my hand on the door and whispered, "Is there anyone in there?" I didn't know if I could help Elizabeth Haunting, or if it was even her trapped in the room, but I thought I should try. I waited but didn't get a response. Some ghosts don't want help, no matter how much you try.

I distract myself by scanning the ghost story book for more Charles Haunting–specific stories. There's a picture of the Paradise Shores grand ballroom. A sudden flash of a waking memory from Mercy's point of view of her dancing with the blond guy, who is very much *not* Nate, plays out in my mind like a movie. Time seems to rewind and stick on that exact moment of Mercy dancing and laughing with the tall, eloquent not-Nate guy. It stops and starts over and over as if I keep hitting the thirty-second rewind button on a remote control. She's comfortable and at ease with not-Nate guy, and, judging by his clothes, he seems like someone who is her social equal or even above her status-wise. He wouldn't be caught dead serving drinks. He's there to see and be seen. He's the type they throw the party for. He's someone like Jay.

"Meredith?" Nathan hesitates as if he's worried about waking me from a dream. "Meredith? What did you see just now?"

I look over at Ritzi, unsure of how much I should say in her presence. She senses my hesitation and waves away my concern. "Hey, we're doing a project on the occult. In this town, the weirder the better, right? Nothing you tell me would surprise me right now."

I point at the ballroom picture in the book in front of me. "I was looking at this picture, and I had a memory. At least I think it was a memory. I've had it before. Mercy and Jay, or at least some guy who reminds me of Jay, were dancing at some sort of party thing. They seemed happy together. She was laughing and smiling and wasn't dancing with him against her will or anything." I watch Nathan for several long, silent moments, but he's careful not to betray any emotion. "It's weird. Whenever I think of them, it's always Mercy-and-Nate or Nate-and-Mercy. I never thought of a third person in the mix, but here he is. Do you think it's possible to be happy with two people at once?"

"If you mean do I think it's possible to love two people at once, then no," Nathan says. "If you mean do I think it's possible Mercy was torn between what her head said was her duty and what her heart said it wanted, then yes. In case you didn't notice, Meredith, you're repeating that same mistake now."

I bristle at his suggestion. "Who says it's such a mistake? You? What do you know?"

"I know Mercy was unhappy, and you're right on track to follow in her footsteps."

Ritzi gathers up a bunch of books. She looks embarrassed. I'm not sure if her embarrassment is for me getting into an argument with Nathan over something he knows nothing about, or for herself for being dropped in the middle of an argument. "I, uh, think I better go." She plans an exit strategy like a champ. "True local ghost stories are our angle, right? I'll see what I can find in these books. See you guys later." She leaves as fast as she can, tripping over her own feet to get out of the library.

Nathan and I stare each other down for several long, tense moments before I say, "Mercy could make up her own mind, and so can I."

"Are you so sure of that?" Nathan challenges. "When was the last time you did something you wanted to do, Meredith, instead of what someone else wanted you to?"

"Before you judge me, Nathan, think about my position and what my father would say. Appearance means everything to him," I remind him. "I can't fight that."

"You mean, you don't *want* to fight that."

I shake my head no, too tired to argue anymore. "I mean, I can't. Just let it go, okay? I don't want to fight."

He forks both hands through his dark hair. "I know, and I feel like an ass for starting anything. I think it's residual Nate-ness bubbling up. On the plus side, we scared off Ritzi."

I reach across the table and swat at his arm. "Be nice. She likes you, you jerk."

Nathan widens his eyes until he looks like a lemur. "Seriously? Says who?"

"Says Ritzi." I lean back in my chair. "That was my fun-filled walk over here. Fielding questions about your relationship status is about the last topic on my list of things I want to talk about."

"I bet that was super awkward." Nathan grins. "I kind of wish I was there to see that. Next time take a video."

"Just be nice to her, okay?" I request. "I'd hate for her to get hurt because you're all single-minded, focused on me when I'm not really available."

"Ah, 'not really available' means you might be available." Nathan jots down research notes before looking up with an innocent smile. "I'm patient. I can wait."

I shake my head, though I'm not really mad—I just have to play the part. If I'm being honest, his persistence gives me hope that I'll be able to break out of my box sooner rather than later. If he believes in me, maybe I can believe in myself. "That's not what I meant."

"How about that you, me, and that cup of coffee we talked about?" Nathan asks. "We don't even have to call it a date since, as you're so fond of pointing out, you have a boyfriend who also happens to be my roommate."

"You don't give up, do you?"

"I'm just happy to be around you," he says. "You talk about missing puzzle pieces. I've already found mine."

How can I stay mad at him when he says stuff like that?

"I'd like to go get coffee, but I don't think that's such a good idea," I say. "Jay wouldn't like it."

"Forget Jay. What would Meredith like?"

I shake my head again, my ponytail swishing against my shoulders with the motion. "Don't go there again, Nathan. I'm tired. Please just accept my decision. I'm sorry if you don't agree with it, but it's mine to make."

He looks like he wants to say more but bites his bottom lip to keep it in, which I appreciate. "At least let me walk you back to the dorms. Would Jay be okay with that?"

No, but I say yes anyway.

Instead of saying goodbye at his floor, Nathan sees me to the third floor. We stand outside my door, neither willing to say goodbye, though we really should. I realize that I'm using Nathan to distract me from all the questions swirling around in my mind. Who is the blond guy I keep seeing in these new waking memories? Could he be the past's version of Jay? Is it more proof that we really are repeating the patterns of the past in the present?

"Are you sure you don't want to grab that cup of coffee?" Nathan offers. "It's not too late. I promise to have you back before the dorms go on lockdown."

As much as I try to play indifferent, I can't help but smile. "I can't, but it is tempting."

"Well, it's better than a no. I'll take it for now." Nathan sticks his hands in his pockets and slouches a little. Finally, he speaks again. Strangely—or maybe not, considering how much seems to piling up in the can't-just-write-off-as-coincidence category—Nathan says what I'm thinking. "I hope you find the answers you're looking for tomorrow, Meredith. I really do."

"So do I, Nathan," I say. "So do I."

Psychic Square is the kind of place that kids around Haunting have been telling stories about for as long as they could drive themselves there or con someone with a car into doing it for them. On the surface, it looks like a quaint little touristy village, like something out of the turn of the century or an alpine mountain village. When Mom was alive, she loved to drive down there on the weekend and check out the custom-made jewelry, learn about the healing power of the various crystals and metals used, and get a psychic reading. Dad is like Jay and about as "show me the science and hard facts before I believe" as they come, so Mom always said the psychic readings and trips to Psychic Square were our little secret. I've never told Dad. I've never told Jay. The trips Mom and I took to Psychic Square are the last little bit of her that is just mine.

Besides the shops, the community graveyard is the place to be on Halloween. Everyone who goes comes back with a "guess what weird and/or creepy thing happened to me in Psychic Square!" story. I've never been brave enough to go, though, to be fair, no one's asked me to tag along either. Halloween is not a fun time of year if you're sensitive to the other side. Haunting is already overactive. Halloween ratchets that activity level up times a thousand. Once I lost Mom, I lost all interest in coming out to Psychic Square. I'm not thrilled about it now either, but I figure, in a whole community populated by psychics, someone can point Nathan and me in the right direction for help. As much as I hate to admit it, we need answers about the dreams and why they're bleeding over to when we're awake.

The knock on my door tells me Jay and Nathan are up as early as I am. Jay shoves a fast food bag at my face when I open the door. Nathan waits behind Jay but doesn't say anything to me.

"We're eating breakfast on the road," Jay says to explain why I have a bag full of breakfast muffin sandwiches under my nose. "No use hanging around waiting for the dining hall to open." Jay slides his sunglasses on. "Let's hit the road and get this over with. Ready to go to Spooky Town USA, Mer?"

I grab my grubby gym shoes since they are the first ones my hands touch and wiggle my feet in. I'll tie them in the car. When Jay's in a hurry, nothing else matters. "Ready. Let's get this over with."

Psychic Square is ninety minutes outside of Haunting. I ride in the front next to Jay, and Nathan sits in the back. At first, we drive in silence, content to munch on our breakfast sandwiches. That gets boring really quick.

"Jay, can't you turn on the radio or something?" I ask. "I need a distraction."

"Here's a thought," Nathan pipes up from the back seat. "Why don't we talk to each other? There's a lot to say, don't you think?"

"Not really," Jay says. "I never have much to say to you, Vale."

"Likewise, Jameson."

"If you boys argue the whole ride, I'll get out and walk home," I warn. "And don't think I won't."

"Don't get mad at me," Jay protests. "Vale's the one that starts it.

You act like he's all innocent, but what do we know about him besides he took a swan dive off the second floor of the rotunda last week? Not a whole lot, that's what."

I look over my shoulder at Nathan lounging in the backseat. "Jay's got a point. You don't talk about yourself at all."

"There's not much to tell," Nathan says. "I grew up in the foster system. I bounced around from home to home. I'll spare you the details of that. The less I remember about that, the better. I worked my butt off to get this scholarship. Coming to Haunting feels like a fresh start. We're all a little broken, just in different ways."

I reach out my hand to Nathan to show my support. He takes it with a grateful smile. "I'm sorry, Nathan. I didn't know about the foster system stuff."

"How could you if I didn't tell you?"

"I just wish there was more I could do."

He shrugs it off. "Don't worry about it. I try not to anymore."

Jay cranks up the radio and guns the engine. It takes ten extra minutes before I realize I'm still holding Nathan's hand. I give it one final squeeze before I untangle my fingers from his. My hand still tingles long after the warmth of his hand leaves mine. I'm lucky Jay didn't notice. It's one instance I'm glad he can be Captain Oblivious.

Halfway to Psychic Square, Jay makes a pit stop for drinks and munchies. It's also a good time to stretch our legs after being cramped in the small car for almost an hour. Nathan and I climb out and head toward the convenience store. Jay is about to follow when his phone rings. I stop to wait. He looks down at the caller ID.

"It's Coach," he says. "I better take this. You go inside. If I don't make it, grab me a soda and chips. You know what I like."

"You sure?" The good girlfriend side of me feels horrible that I'm using Jay for his car and then ignoring him all morning. "I can wait."

He waves me inside, mouthing "go" as he clicks the accept call button. "Hey, Coach, what's up? Yeah, sure, I have time to talk strategy. No, I don't care it's Saturday. Go ahead. I'm listening."

I meet up with Nathan in the chip aisle. He's balanced an insane number of snacks and cold drinks in his arms. He lifts his arms to show off his haul. "I wasn't sure what you wanted, so I just picked one of everything."

I laugh. "We might want to put some of that back."

"There're a lot of things we might want to do, but putting back my snacks is not one of them."

I look around for Jay because I always expect him to show up when I'm alone with Nathan—especially when he's talking all intense. *There're a lot of things we might want to do.* What does that even mean?

"Why do you always do that?" I ask. "I mean, I get the 'life is too short to not go after what you want' philosophy, but I'm not available. You know this, but you keep making all these comments. You don't even bother to show any tact around Jay. You just say everything you're feeling."

"Does that make you uncomfortable?" Nathan sets down his snacks and soda and takes my hand. His palm is sweaty and cold all at once, but it still sends little electric shivers down my arm, through my body, and straight down to my toes. I suck in my breath, trying to ignore the sensation. "'Cause, you know, Mer, every time you mention having a boyfriend, it comes across to me like an excuse not to face how you really feel. It's easier to stick to what you know versus really figuring things out. Don't you owe it to yourself to figure things out before you're stuck any further in a life you might not want, let alone like?"

I close my eyes and try to imagine what it would be like if I called the shots for once instead of Dad or Jay, but all I get is a big blank. "It seems like my whole life has been one big confusion," I admit. "I don't know how to change that."

"Maybe now is the perfect time to start."

As if it is no longer accepting orders from my brain, my hand moves to caress Nathan's cheek. My fingers move back and forth, back and forth. I watch as if they belong to someone else's hand. Nathan closes his eyes and leans into my palm.

"Meredith."

My name on his lips holds such longing and promise that I almost drop everything in my arms to follow wherever it may lead me.

Almost.

My head retakes control, just in time. This is a dangerous game our emotions are playing—one I can't play now, or ever. I pull away and gather up my snacks and drinks.

"Jay will send a search party for us if we don't get back to the car." I keep my voice casual. "Come on; I'll buy the snacks."

"You can't avoid talking to me forever, Meredith," Nathan says as he follows me to the front of the store.

"I'm not avoiding talking to you." I load the counter with our snack and drink selections and try to focus on the beep-beeping of the cash register as the clerk rings everything up. "I'm avoiding talking about my private life, that's all. Anything about Jay and me is off-limits. Don't push, Nathan. If you do, I can guarantee you will not like the consequences."

"If that's what you want." Nathan looks like he wants to say more but stays silent as we head back to Jay's Camaro and pile in. In less than an hour, we'll be at Psychic Square. Maybe we'll find answers, maybe we won't, but, no matter what, we've got to try. Maybe whatever answers we find will help settle whatever's happening between Nathan and me. We need to try.

The closer we get to Psychic Square, the more nervous I feel. On the outside, we're just another batch of tourists. On the inside, I know this is more than just a fun afternoon road trip.

"It's not as bad as I thought it would be," Jay says once we find parking near the town center where the shops and businesses cluster. "It's kind of cool, I guess. It reminds me of Main Street in Haunting."

"But more specialized," I add. "Main Street only has one metaphysical shop. This is like Main Street times a thousand."

"Do you really need more than one metaphysical shop?" Jay glances around at the shop signs and window displays. Crystal healings, tarot readings, Reiki healings, angel cards, hand-crafted spiritual jewelry, Akashic records, psychic medium, hypnotherapy. You name it, someone at Psychic Square specializes in it. "Even if I believed in psychic powers, it seems a little tacky to be pimping yourself out as a medium."

"Maybe they feel the need to share their gift." Nathan looks over at me as if to say, "Your secret is safe with me." He won't tell Jay or anyone else that my "I see dead people" ability makes me a medium—

the very thing Jay just called tacky. "Having a connection to the other side is a talent like anything else. Did you ever stop to think that if you turned pro after graduation, you'd be 'pimping yourself out' to companies for endorsement deals?"

"That's different!" Jay protests. "Endorsement deals are how pro athletes make most of their money."

"And charging for readings is how mediums make theirs," Nathan says.

"You're just as whack-a-doo as Meredith for believing in all this new-age mumbo jumbo crap," Jay says. "For all you know, your all-knowing, all-seeing medium could've stolen your wallet and gone through it for information. Remind me again why I even bothered to come along?"

"You're welcome to stay in the car." Nathan heads toward the cluster of shops, and I follow.

"And leave you alone with Meredith?" Jay hurries to catch up. "Not a chance."

"How will we know we pick the right person to help us?" I turn around in a circle to get a good look at all the names on the shops. "There're so many signs and names and doors. How will we know which one is the right one?"

"Oh, believe me, we'll know." Nathan sounds a lot more confident than I feel. "Sometimes, you have to trust fate instead of fact."

A door creaks open to our right, and we all turn to look. A little old lady, with dyed bright red-orange hair and wearing more eyeshadow and smeared red lipstick than any one person has any business putting on at once, steps out of the shop door. She takes one look at the three of us, and her red-smeared mouth breaks into a grin.

"I knew you'd come," she says as if welcoming three wayward grandchildren home for cookies and milk. "Just this morning I was talking to Mercy and Nate, and they said you'd come. They said the time was now and to expect you this afternoon—12:01 sharp." She taps the gold watch hanging off her boney wrist. "12:01 sharp."

"Whack-a-doo," Jay whispers close to my ear while Nathan looks around like he expects her to be talking to someone else on the deserted street, but Granny Lady has already said the magic words to make me take an involuntary step forward.

Mercy and Nate.

"May I ask how you know about Mercy and Nate?" I ask.

"Oh, honey, I know everything about Mercy and Nate," Little Old Psychic Granny Lady says. "You look every bit like her. I knew you would. If I didn't know any better, I would say Mercy Stone was standing before me now instead of a scared, uncertain school girl."

It's the first time I've heard Mercy's last name. "Can you help us?" I take another step closer as if afraid she'll disappear and leave us with even more questions than we came with. "I'm Meredith. This is Nathan and Jay. We're looking for answers, but I think you already know that. Please, can you help us?"

Little Old Psychic Granny Lady grins at me before turning the wattage toward Nathan. "Oh, children, I'm so happy you came. I knew you would because Mercy and Nate never lie to me. I have so much to tell you. There's so much to share."

"We've been having strange dreams." Nathan's voice is halting like he suddenly thinks she of all people will think he's strange. "They've moved over into when we're awake now. We can't shake them. I don't think we're meant to. There's something we're missing in them. Some lesson we forgot to learn. Can you help us find answers?"

Little Old Psychic Granny Lady nods before opening her door and motioning us all inside. I glance at the sign above as we pass into the threshold—*Myrtle Stone King: Medium and Tarot*. She catches me reading the sign and nods.

"Isn't it funny how Fate and the Universe deal us such hands? We can correct even one-hundred-twenty-year-old mistakes if we know the workings of the soul."

"Mistakes?" I ask. "What kind of mistakes?"

Mrs. King pats my hand. "Oh, child, you'll find that out in time."

Jay is the last to enter the shop. A little bell jingles as Mrs. King shuts the door behind us. Mrs. King has decorated her shop with various vintage paintings and furniture. Lavender and sandalwood incense is burning while soothing meditation-style music plays.

"It smells." Jay looks around the cluttered, incense-heavy shop.

Mrs. King laughs. "Oh, James was always such a skeptic too. Even in a town and time where the occult was all the rage, he only cared about money and social appearances. It seems some things never change."

"Yeah, whatever, lady," Jay mutters under his breath, which only makes her smile all the more.

"I dusted off all my old albums today." Mrs. King sits down at a round table and motions for us to take seats opposite her. "I knew you'd come, so I wanted to prepare." She turns the heavy, yellowed photo album so that it faces us before she opens it. The first sepia-toned picture is of a girl about my age, wearing one of those fancy dresses with a bustle that debutants made their society debuts in. She piled her hair up on her head, but a few curls escaped down her neck for effect. I hear Nathan's breath hiss through his teeth beside me, and I know he sees it too.

Her face.

Her face is my face.

"Where did you get this?" My throat is so constricted I'm surprised I can even speak above a croak.

"This is Mercy Stone." Mrs. King taps the picture with one long red fingernail. "My great-aunt."

I search Mrs. King's wrinkled face, looking for any resemblance to the girl in the picture—the girl with my face. I think it must be a little sad and more than a little frustrating to grow older and watch your body break down while your mind and spirit stay young. Mom always said that the eyes are the window to the soul. Mrs. King's eyes are bright blue, like two sparkling sapphires, but, more than that, they're kind. I can trust her. I know I can.

"Great-aunt?" I say. "I don't understand."

"My grandmother was barely out of the pram when Mercy died, but they raised her on the stories of The Incident." Mrs. King sighs. "There are so many stories. So many hearts broken." She sighs again and shakes her head as if she's reliving memories she was never a part of. Maybe Mercy and Nate told her the truth, just like the truth is trying to get out through my and Nate's dreams. Mrs. King runs her fingers down Mercy's picture. "It's tragic how one decision can break so many hearts and cause so many ripples that are felt all the way to today. Mercy. Nate. My great-grandparents. Even James felt it, though I'm sure he'd never admit to it."

Jay makes a noise that I can't tell if it's meant to be in derision or approval. Mrs. King raises her eyes from the photo book to look at him.

"I can tell you have much in common with James Piper." Mrs. King flips to the next page in the album. "Very much indeed."

A young man—older than Mercy—dressed in a dark three-piece suit stares back at us from the photo album page as if daring us to question him, question his motives, and question his money that gives him the right and privilege to look so entitled. He has Jay's light hair, and, though the picture is the same sepia tone as the one before, I'm guessing he also has Jay's ice-blue eyes.

"Dude, do you believe in any of this now?" Nathan asks Jay. "This just proves we made the right decision by coming here today."

"It's easy to photoshop pictures nowadays." Jay dismisses the resemblance. "I bet she scanned one of my 'Jay Jameson wins again' pictures from the paper and had her grandkids photoshop it. Same with the one of you, Mer." He gestures at the album. "Our picture was in the paper when we went to the spring cotillion last year, remember? Anyone with even an ounce of tech-savvy can scan and photoshop these days. I don't know how she found out we were coming, maybe Vale tipped her off or something to impress you, but showing off pictures that look like they came from that that Old-Time Photo store won't convince me of anything."

"Can't you admit for just one second that you're not always right about everything?" Nathan snaps. "Maybe, just maybe, there are things you don't know or are beyond the realm of scientific understanding. I don't have all the answers either, but I at least have an open mind. Try it sometime, Jameson. If you don't..." Nathan trails off.

I put my hand on Jay's arm to stop him from jumping over Mrs. King's table and going after Nathan. "Jay," I warn. "Seriously, why do I have to remind you boys to calm down whenever we're all together? This is not funny or cute or exciting or any way else you can think to describe it. It's obnoxious and immature. Grow up a little—both of you."

"Vale started it," Jay insists.

"Oh, like that's real mature?" Nathan laughs. "Good one, Jameson. Just think about the open-mind thing. If you don't, I'm not responsible for what might happen."

I step in front of Jay this time to hold him back. I put my hands on his chest and push him back into a chair. "That's enough, Jay! Can you stop acting like an ass for one second and realize that I *want* to be here? I want to be here, okay? This was my idea. You have the car, yes, but it was my idea to come here. I need answers, and Mrs. King can help me. I know she can. You can believe whatever you want to believe, and so can I. I believe she can help me. That she can help us. Please don't belittle that or me with your bad attitude."

Jay pushes himself away from the chair in one angry, fluid motion. "This is bogus. I'm waiting in the car. Don't come crying to me when Psychic Granny rips you off. I'm betting her 'answers' and 'help' come with a price tag."

The bell on the door jangles for Jay's exit as it did for his entrance. I turn to Mrs. King once he's gone. "I'm sorry, ma'am. We shouldn't have brought Jay along. As you can tell, he's not really into things that numbers or science can't explain."

"I wouldn't expect any less from a young man who is very much like James," she murmurs before flipping to the next page in the photo album. "History likes to repeat itself in your cases, my children, doesn't it?"

On the album page facing us, an old, half-faded newspaper clipping declares PARADISE SHORES RE-OPENS FOR THE SEASON next to a grainy picture of an elegant hotel that looks similar to all the others from this era. My eyes track the article, not even reading, in search of something I knew must be there.

"There."

I point at a group picture toward the bottom of the page over the caption THE STAFF IS WAITING TO WELCOME YOU. Maids, kitchen staff, elevator operators, and gardeners all jumble together for the group shot, but I can't take my eyes off of one face in particular. Dressed in dark pants and a white high collar jacket, with his dark hair slicked back with a little too much pomade, is the boy from my dreams and waking visions. The boy with Nathan's face.

"Nate," I whisper as my fingertip caresses his blurry cheek. "You're real."

"Was real," Nathan corrects. "He died, remember? They all died."

"And so very young," Mrs. King adds. "It's such a shame when someone wastes young love and young lives."

"Can you tell us what happened?" I look up from the old newspaper clipping and search her creased face for any clues to the past—clues I now want to run toward instead of away from.

She shakes her head. "You discovered me, but I can only point you in the right direction for the answers you seek. It's not my story to tell, but theirs." She stands and rummages through a stack of papers on a smaller end table off to her right. "It's here somewhere. I know it is. Ah! Perfect!" Mrs. King turns around, holding a beige card in her hand, and presents it to us. "Go to Catalina. She can help you from here."

"Help us how?" Nathan asks as he reads the business card over my shoulder. *Open Closed Doors to find the truth of your soul.*

"Catalina is a hypnotherapist," Mrs. King says. "She can help you unlock the secrets of your soul's past to heal the present. You *do* want to heal the present and stop the one-hundred-twenty-year cycle of heartache, don't you?" She raises her dyed red-orange eyebrows at us as if to say, *Why would you not?*

"Like fixing a mistake so we learn from it instead of doing it over again?" I ask.

Mrs. King smiles and nods. "Exactly. Though, to be fair, Mercy and Nate were very much a product of their time. They tried to buck society's traditions and confines, but it proved too great for them. I only hope that, if you face the same choice, you will learn from it instead of succumbing to it. No one should be unhappy, and your souls have been aching with unhappiness for over a century." She taps the business card in my hand. "That's why you need to go to Catalina. She can help."

"So, let me see if I got this right," Nathan begins. "You're saying the reason we're having all these dreams and visions is our souls have unfinished business, and we need to go to this Catalina person to work it out? What happens when we find out what happened in the past? We're aware that bad stuff happened, and that somehow means we won't make the same mistake over again?"

"Smart boy." Mrs. King pats his cheek like she knows him, and I guess she thinks she does. "By understanding past-life mistakes, you can see your current hurtful soul-patterns and break them." She taps the card in my hand again with one long painted fingernail. "Go to Catalina. She will help you."

"Thank you," I say since I don't know what else is appropriate. "How much do I owe you, Mrs. King?"

She waves a hand as I unzip my purse in search of my wallet. "Put your money away, child. For Mercy and Nate, I would do anything. You can't put a price on correcting soul-patterns, my dear."

"Can I at least give you a donation?" I hold my wallet in my hands, ready for her to name her price.

"Just promise me you won't forget me or this day and that you'll break the patterns of the past. That's all the payment that I need."

"We promise," Nathan and I say together.

His hand snakes down to grasp mine, squeezing tight, and I feel the same little electric shock shoot through me like I did at the gas station. I squeeze back, taking courage from the gesture of support and solidarity. We came looking for answers today, but I know this is only the beginning. I glance down at the business card in my hand again. Open Closed Doors. My breath catches in my throat when I notice the address.

"Oh no."

"What?" Nathan is on alert. "What is it?"
"Catalina's office is next to the graveyard in Haunting."

Chapter 16

"I believe the graveyard is in a lovely location, miss." Abigail putters around my room, straightening things that don't need straightening. No matter how many times I tell her not to do it, old habits die hard. Almost a whole week has passed, and I still haven't got up the courage to call Catalina or go into the shop to book an appointment. "Why are you so afraid to go to a shop right next door? Especially if you're bound to find your answers there."

"It's not so much the graveyard itself, but who hangs out there," I say. "It's probably the only place in town fuller of restless ghosts than the school."

Abigail shrugs. "Is that such a bad thing? Maybe they need your help."

"I can only handle one project at a time." I stuff some books and notebooks into my backpack. I need to meet Nathan and Ritzi in the library to work on our Colorado History project. Local ghost stories and séance practices are our go-to topics right now. At least it's a good topic if we need an excuse for why we're hanging around near the graveyard once I do get up the courage to go Open Closed Doors. That's convenient.

"Maybe another time," Abigail says.

"Maybe." I don't want to commit to being some go-to-the-light crusader. I'd rather just keep my head down, do my school work, and act as normal as possible. I already feel like I'm living a double life as it is with the possible past-life memories. Do I want to add helping ghosts into the mix?

I walk alone to the library. I expected Ritzi to knock on the door and get me, but she's been acting a little weird in class. She's been peppy and sociable. She's always been friendly, but it's almost like she's hiding something behind this new persona. She might just be trying to get Nathan's attention by being the fun, vibrant, center-of-attention girl she thinks he wants, but I'm not buying it. There's something Ritzi is not telling us. I just don't know what it is.

If she's just trying to get Nathan to notice her, that bit is working. He's been talking to Ritzi more and me less in class this last week. Part of me is happy he's taking an interest in someone other than me, while a big part of me that has no right to be jealous is just that— completely envious. I hate it, but white-hot anger flares in my stomach every time he smiles at Ritzi or compliments one of her project ideas. I'm annoyed when she leans over and whispers to me how cute Nathan is or how she plans to ask him out after class. The jealousy eases up when I'm positive he lets her down with some excuse, but that doesn't stop it from circling back around whenever she turns up the charm all over again. What if she wears Nathan down? What if he decides I'm not worth hanging around for and goes after a girl that's available and very into him? What if, what if, what if? I can't stand it. I'll drive myself crazy if I keep thinking in circles.

Nathan waves me over to the table when I enter the library. Ritzi is already there. She smiles but doesn't look one hundred percent pleased that I've interrupted her alone time with Nathan.

"Hey, what did I miss?" I try to be bright and cheerful, just in case that really is the kind of girl Nathan is looking for. Ugh. What am I thinking? I have a boyfriend. Even if he is sometimes an insecure ass, he is still my boyfriend.

"Ritzi found a book with a great rundown on a Victorian séance," Nathan says. "She thinks it will be a great visual for our project."

"We'll show the class what a séance looked like back in the day." Ritzi blushes a little, looking pleased that Nathan is giving her credit for the suggestion. "Most were fake anyway. They just piggybacked on the whole occult craze. We'll show off the props used and how the medium would make the people think they were really taking to the dead. I think having the visual will be really amazing."

I frown. "As long as you don't call up any real spirits. If you're into the metaphysical, you know how crowded this town is with restless energy."

"Oh, I know." Ritzi dismisses my concern as if I'd said, "Hey, read chapter two before the test tomorrow." She even waves her hand a little. "Trust me," she continues. "I'll be careful."

"You better be," I say. "The alternative is not an option."

Nathan looks over at me and raises both eyebrows. I shake my head and mouth "later." The less he knows the destruction that can happen by calling malevolent spirits, the better.

"Hey, Meredith, why don't you help me put some of these books back?" Nathan stands and loads me down with books. I know it's an excuse to get me alone so we can talk about going to Open Closed Doors. I play along by following him deep into the book stacks.

"So, I have a plan." Nathan shelves books to make our cover story believable. "Our goal is to find answers to the past by going to Catalina at Open Closed Doors but without Jay and his downer of an attitude tagging along, right?"

"Right," I agree. "I feel he's part of this as much as we are—that picture of James Piper can't be just a coincidence—but I want to feel like I have the freedom to discover Mercy and Nate's story instead of feeling like I need to apologize to Jay for being interested in the past every two seconds." I stick a book on the shelf. "Where are you going with this plan of yours?"

"So, neither of us have a car, the shop is too far to walk to, and I don't want to be tied to the bus schedule, so that leaves borrowing a car." Nathan grimaces. "I hate to even say it but, uh, what would you have to do in order borrow Jay's car?"

"Are you on crack?" I shove a book into the shelf and knock three more out. I pick them up and try again. "That's a horrible plan. No one just 'borrows' Jay's car. That car is his baby. It means more to him than I do. It means maybe more to him than me and all his ski trophies combined. No one just borrows his car. Nothing I can say or do will change that."

Nathan puts his hand over mine where it rests on the spine of a book. "Are you sure? You can't think of any way to change his mind?"

"I can, but you won't like the answer."

Nathan puffs his cheeks out like he's about to vomit. "You're right. Don't do that. Ever. At least not with him."

"Any other bright ideas?

"All I know is we need to learn from our mistakes, not repeat them. I'm trying to do that by figuring out a way to get us to Catalina's shop without Mr. Buzzkill tagging along. I know you think you're just doing your duty by dating him, but—guess what—that's what Mercy thought she was doing, and where did that land her? Do you remember?"

"Dead."

I don't mean to say it. I don't think I even know the answer to Nathan's question, but there it is—the single word that can explain all my constant, churning dread at the outcome of this pushing and pulling, head-versus-heart drama I've somehow got myself into and somehow seem just as unwilling to get myself out of.

"Dead." I repeat it as if testing the finality of the word. *Dead.*

"Exactly, and that's the last thing I want to see happen to you—not if I can help it this time around. I called Catalina at Open Closed Doors. There's an opening tomorrow afternoon. We could leave after class." Nathan digs around in his back pocket and produces what looks like paperwork. "We must get these permission and liability forms filled out first. It's okay to be scared, Meredith. I'm scared too. But even though I'm scared, I still think we owe it to ourselves to do this. We need to do this for us, for Nate and Mercy, and for everyone involved. We owe it to ourselves to find answers and learn their full story. The dreams and visions only tell part of it. We need to know the whole truth."

I take the papers he offers. "I'll see if Jay will loan us his car or maybe drive and wait outside. I can't guarantee anything, but I'll try."

Nathan's shoulders sag in relief. "Thanks. I know it's a lot to ask of you. I appreciate that you're willing to try. Call or text me after you've talked to Jay, okay?"

I nod before I shelve the last book. "It may be late."

"I don't mind," he says. "Just promise me you'll call."

"I promise, but don't expect a miracle."

"I won't." Nathan flashes me a grin before heading back to our library table.

After he's gone, I take out my cell phone to text Jay: *Meet me @ our spot. 911.*

"What's the emergency?" Jay is out of breath from sprinting up the stairs to the Widow's Walk. "I came as soon as I read your text."

"Sorry," I apologize. "I shouldn't have texted 911. It's not really that much of an emergency."

"Don't scare me like that, Mer." Jay sits down next to me on the rooftop of Widow's Walk, still working on calming his breathing. Whenever we need a quiet place just to chill and relax or talk, we always come here. We've seen so many sunsets and sunrises from this roof. We shared our first kiss here. He gave me my Claddagh ring here. We've built years of memories here, and all of them are good. Jay and I may have our rough patches, especially as I struggle to decide if I still want to be his girlfriend and Daddy's good girl that never goes against what is expected. No matter how confused I feel, I wouldn't trade any of my memories with Jay. Not for a second.

"Did Nathan ever join the ski team as an alternate?" I ask.

Jay makes the same vomit face that Nathan made in the library. "Can we please go ten seconds without talking about Vale? It's bad enough I have to share a room with the guy. I don't need you fangirling all over him too."

"Fangirling?" I sit up straighter, surprised by his word choice. "Is that what you think I'm doing?"

"Well, aren't you?" Jay asks. "I get it, though. He's new and exciting. You've seen me every day since you were twelve, and we've been dating for two years. I'm old news." Jay ruffles a hand through his blond hair, giving it a casual messiness. I love it, though have never told him so. "Would it be weird if I said I was half-expecting something like this to happen someday? Maybe that's why I've been acting like such an ass. I guess the only variable I didn't know in the whole equation was the who and when. Now I know. Now I can plug all the variables in and that scares me. No, it more than scares me, Meredith, it terrifies me."

I scoot over until I'm sitting in his lap with my back against his chest, our legs stretched out with mine on top of his. Jay wraps his arms around my waist. I lay my hands on top of his where they rest near my hips and trace circles on the back of his hands with my fingertips. "I didn't know you felt that way, Jay."

"Yeah, well, it's kind of a bitch when you can see your girlfriend slipping away from you right in front of your eyes. It makes me act out, so sue me." He tightens his arms before loosening them again. "Why can't we stay like this forever, Mer? Why can't we just run off to a cabin in the mountains somewhere and just forget about everyone else?"

I close my eyes and imagine what it would be like to run away from everything and just be Meredith and Jay. No school, no ski team, no Dad, only us. It wouldn't be a bad life. Maybe there'd be no great romance-novel passion, but I'd be secure, happy, and loved. There's nothing wrong with a quiet love. All-consuming passion gets you killed in classic literature, anyway. "Tempting, but the real world doesn't work that way, Jay."

"Why not? We can make it work. We can make anything work as long as we're together." Jay turns me so that I'm facing him, my legs straddling his upper thighs. My arms go up around his neck, and I press against his chest.

"Are you kidding?" I try to joke away my importance in his life. "You'd have a thousand girls lined up to take my place if I was out of the picture."

"I don't want a thousand girls, Meredith, I just want you."

I kiss him. Jay is so surprised, he falls backward, and I land on top of him. A kiss may not seem all that spontaneous, but, for me, queen of keeping my emotions, thoughts, and feelings under wraps, it is a very, very impulsive act.

"What was that for?" Jay asks when I pull away. "Not that I'm complaining, but usually you're all into the ice-princess routine—at least in public—so I guess I thought it would bleed over into private. Do that again."

I kiss him again. I rest my head against his chest and listen to his heart beating. "I'm sorry I've neglected you—that I've neglected us. It's just that I've had a lot on my mind. I know that's not an excuse, and you have every right to be mad at me, but I wanted you to know I feel horrible about it too. I really do."

"It's okay." Jay is quick to forgive, though I'm not sure how fast he'll be to forget. "We can try harder now. I've had a lot on my mind too with ski season and graduation looming. I've told no one this, but I don't know what I'll do after graduation."

I sit up, and we get back into regular sitting position instead of draped all over each other. To be honest, I miss his warmth. I grab his hand to hold on to his closeness a little while longer. "What are you talking about? You'll go pro. Everyone knows that."

"Yeah, I know, but it's not like skiing is a year-round job. What do I do with the rest of my time? I guess I can work for my dad, but I'd like something that's just mine and not forced on me, you know?"

I squeeze Jay's hand. "I know how you feel."

We're silent, watching the stars blink into view. I allow myself to enjoy the moment for as long as I can. I know asking to borrow the car will destroy the fragile understanding we've rediscovered, but I have to ask it now, or I'll lose my nerve. I need to speak out. I need to have my voice heard. I don't want to be a silent doormat of a person forever.

"Jay? Can I ask you something?"

"Anything." He leans over and kisses the top of my head.

"I need to borrow your car tomorrow after class so I can go to a past-life regression appointment in town." He opens his mouth, lips forming the word "no," so I plow on before he gets the protest out. "You don't have to come with. I know you don't believe in all this new-age, fate's-hand-at-work stuff, but I need to see if it's true or not. I need to know, Jay. You can understand that, right? I feel like my life is a puzzle with pieces missing. I want to find the missing pieces. With this appointment, it feels like one of those pieces is dangling in front of me. I need to grab it while I can. I need to fill everything in so I can see the big picture."

"And if I say yes?" Jay's eyes go squinty like he's trying to gauge my real reason for asking. "What then?"

"If you say yes, I get my answers, I find my puzzle pieces, and we get back on with normal life." I scoot closer until I press my left side to his right and lay my head on his shoulder. "I know it's a lot to ask, Jay. I'm sorry if it's too much. I know what your car means to you."

"Is Vale going with?"

"Of course Nathan is going with. He's a part of this," I say. "You're a part of it too, Jay, even if you don't want to admit it or have any part in it. Mrs. King didn't doctor those photos. They were real. This is *all* real. We need to figure out why it's happening to us. That's why we need to go to this appointment tomorrow after class."

"I'm coming if he's coming," Jay insists.

Jealousy. I should have guessed earlier jealousy is the best way to get Jay to agree to my and Nathan's plan.

"I'm not leaving you or my car alone with him," he adds.

"Thank you, Jay." I decide not to acknowledge the flare of jealousy I hear in his voice. "I appreciate you helping us out. I appreciate you. Even if I don't always say it or show it as much as I should, I really do appreciate you."

Jay stands before pulling me to my feet. "It's settled then. We get this done, and things go back to the way they were before. Tell Vale to meet me in the parking lot tomorrow afternoon. I hope you find your answers, Mer. I really do."

"Thanks. I hope so too."

Jay slings an arm around my shoulders and pulls me close as we climb down from the Widow's Walk roof and back to the dorms. It's past seven, so he can't come onto my floor. We say goodnight at the grand staircase instead. I wave and blow him one final kiss as I disappear through the locking staircase door. On my climb to the third floor, I suddenly feel scared instead of excited to explore the past. *This is what you want*, I tell myself. *No, more than that. This is what you need.*

True to his word, Jay is waiting for Nathan and me in the parking lot after classes finish the next day. He doesn't look happy about going, but he's here and not complaining (for now). Just like the drive to Psychic Square, I climb in the front seat, Nathan slips into the back seat, and we're off.

The layout of the town of Haunting is a little weird. The hotel-turned-school and surrounding historical district are separated by downtown and the lake by several miles. It's too far to walk between them, though I know some people who bike or bus. Despite Jay's less-than-sunny disposition and the horrendous state of parking downtown, it's just easier to drive, in our case. Parking of any kind in downtown Haunting is hard to find. You might as prepare to sell your soul if you want free parking. The best-kept, free-parking secret that only the locals know about is next to the rec center tennis court. It's a little bit of a hike to Main Street where Open Closed Doors is, but it's worth it to avoid the annoying tourist pay-by-the-hour parking lots, and the even more annoying tourists who ask anyone who looks like they may be a resident for directions to the graveyard or where to sign up for ghost tours.

"You've been stuck on campus since you got here." Jay turns to Nathan after we park by the tennis courts, acknowledging his presence for the first time since we started the short trip across town. I notice a new edge to his voice. Even though he's trying to control it, it feels like he expects Nathan and me to mug him, steal his car keys, and drive off into the sunset together. "Have you ever been to downtown?"

Nathan shakes his head. "It seems familiar like I could find my way around if you asked me to. Maybe I watched a tourist video with my application packet or something."

Or maybe we all lived here in the 1800s, I want to say but don't. We'll find that out soon enough.

We walk in the graveyard's direction and, by extension, Open Closed Doors to make it to our appointment on time. I walk in the middle of the boys because the more space between them, the better. The buildings on Main Street look almost identical to any other street you may walk down in the heart of Haunting with its mix of Victorian and Edwardian architecture. They rise from the sidewalk close together, giving the impression of row houses on the East Coast like Boston or New York. Since many of the turn-of-the-century inhabitants were from the East Coast, it makes sense they would want their houses to look like the ones they left behind. In present times, any building near the pedestrian shopping district of Main Street is someone's home and business. The business is on the ground floor, and the apartment is on top. Open Closed Doors looks like it's no different.

There's no bell to signal our entrance when we step inside, but the waiting area is small enough that we shouldn't have an issue getting the receptionist's attention.

"Very Feng Shui," Jay comments as we glance around the decorated reception room with its black leather couches, low wood tables, potted plants, and framed Chinese symbol artwork on the walls.

The receptionist looks ten years older than us, max. She looks up when we come in, watching us with the same "I knew you would come" blasé attitude Mrs. King sported when she found us in Psychic Square. She's dressed all in black with silver pentacle earrings and a matching necklace. Her hair is the bright pink of an anime character.

"May I help you?" she asks.

Nathan does the talking for us. "We scheduled an appointment with Catalina for a past-life regression session." He takes the permission forms out of his backpack and lays them on the counter. "We got these signed too."

"I'm Catalina." She stands and moves around the reception desk. She punches a button on the phone to send any incoming calls to voicemail before turning her full attention back to us. "You're welcome to be in the room when I put you under, but I don't do group regressions. My policy is one at a time. It gets too crazy if people interact with each other as their past-life selves. I did that at a regression party once, and it just got too wild. I said to myself, 'never again,' and that was that." She gestures around the store. "Now I just run the shop. None of that off-shoot stuff. I have Meredith and Nathan on the schedule. It doesn't take a psychic to know you're Meredith." Catalina points at me. "Now which one of you handsome young men is Nathan?"

"I am." Nathan taps his chest.

"Gotcha." Catalina gives me a wink as if to say, "Lucky you, escorted by the likes of them." If only she knew being around both boys at the same time was like refereeing World War III. "Now, who would like to go first?"

"I will," I volunteer. I didn't realize I was so ready to get this going until the words come out of my mouth. "It's safe, right? I won't get stuck in the past or anything, will I?"

"Only in horror movies." Catalina motions for us to follow her to the back room. It's decorated much like the outer office with framed art, leather couches, and a recliner. A dark window shade blocks most of the light. Soft music pipes low and soothing from a stereo. I felt safe and comfortable in Mrs. King's shop, and I feel the same way the second we step into this room at Catalina's shop. We can trust her. I can relax here.

"What do I need to do first?" I ask.

"I base hypnosis in relaxation techniques, so the key is being comfortable and free from distractions," Catalina explains. "Pick a couch or recliner—wherever you will feel able to relax."

I pick the recliner. "Do you just snap your fingers, and it's done?"

"Hardly." Catalina sits at a desk I didn't notice before. "I start by guiding your breathing to help you relax, and then we do a deepening technique to take you further under, and, finally, there's visualization. If you have a particular past life in mind, I can't guarantee we'll go there, but I can help try to guide you there if you feel it's affecting your life the most now."

"There is one that I think is being rather, uh, insistent," I say. "I'm having dreams about it, and now it's interfering with my day-to-day life."

"You got that right," Jay mutters, but I ignore him. We're here for my answers. I can't worry about Jay's reaction right now.

Catalina nods and leans back in her own chair. She's got paper and pen in front of her.

"Why are you taking notes?" I ask. "Won't I remember what I see?"

"It's just so you have a paper trail," she clarifies. "You'll remember everything you see and hear during the session. It will be as real as if you were living it except you can't be hurt. You won't feel any physical pain. You'll still feel the emotional connection. I wish there were a way to dull that more."

"What do you need for me to do?"

"Just close your eyes, relax, listen to my voice, and try to follow my instructions."

I nod, close my eyes, and take a deep, calming breath that I can feel in my whole chest. "Okay. I'm ready."

"Let's begin."

Catalina starts off by telling me to focus on my breathing. I feel my body relaxing with every breath, especially when she says, "Breathe in relaxation, breathe out tension." Next, she moves into what's called "the deepening." She asks me to imagine a soothing warmth spreading from the top of my head to the tips of my toes. My eyes and body feel heavy, but in a good way as if I'm about to fall into a deep sleep. Finally, she asks me to visualize taking an elevator down, down, down to a circular room. I picture the library at school. There are books all around, each shelf representing a past life. I'm supposed to pick the one that is affecting me the most in the present. I decide on the third shelf from the bottom. To the right, she says, are positive memories from this life; to the left, negative memories. I'm supposed to pick which I would like to explore. I notice a book lying open in the middle—not positive or negative but somewhere more neutral. I pick it up.

"Can you tell me what year it is?" Catalina's voice penetrates my heavy mind.

"1888," I answer without even thinking.

"Can you tell me your name?"

"Mercy Stone."

"What are you doing now, Mercy?"

"Arguing with Nate," I say. "He is cross with me again."

"Why is he cross with you?"

"Because he says I always do what people expect instead of choosing for myself. He thinks I am being taken advantage of."

"By whom?"

"By everyone," I answer.

"Would you like to tell us more about that?" Catalina asks. "What makes Nate feel that way?"

I pause. "I will try."

"Please. Whenever you are ready."

The pause is longer this time, but the words come. "I am ready."

Haunting, 1888
Mercy Stone

"Oh, *do* stop acting like such a child, Nate!" I scramble down the lake's stone retention wall after him but make quite a mess of it with my heels and restrictive skirt. All I do—besides sound like a petulant child myself—is land in the sand on my hands and knees.

"*I'm* actin' like a child?" He whirls to face me as I pick myself up off the sand and brush off my hands and dress. "You're the one who lets your father or James lead ya about from room to room and gala to gala like a little china doll. When will you learn that you're not just some little thing to dress up and parade about? Why don't ya show some gumption for once, Mercy? I know ya have it in ya. God knows I do, or we wouldn't row as much as we seem to." He leans down until his face is only inches from mine. I cannot decide if I want to slap him or kiss him. "Where is the fire I know is in there, Mercy? Let it out. Be your own person for once in your life."

"It is easier to do as I am told to avoid confrontation," I say. "I show gumption with you, Nate, and look where it gets us—endless rounds of squabbles. Please, do not be cross with me, Nate. Please?" I look him square in the face, trying to memorize every detail of those dear, dear features. Every moment with him feels like our last. I do not know how much longer I can play these games of running off before Papa locks me down to a formal engagement with James. It is a dangerous line I walk. I cannot shirk my duty forever. Unfortunately, my duty is to society and not my heart. As much as I wish and hope otherwise, I just see no way around that painful truth.

Nate sighs before leaning in for a kiss. It is long and lingering as if he is trying to store up memories as well for the inevitable time when we will need to part. "You know I cannot stay cross for long, Mercy." His grin turns mischievous. "No matter how vexing you may be."

I swat at his arm and shove off before stomping over to the water's edge. I watch the water lap at my bare feet. How wonderful would it be to be born to another station in life so I could be free to decide my fate. Instead, I am like the doll Nate accused me of being. I am only expected to dress up and look pretty on James's arm. The emptier my head, the better.

"I know you believe me a frivolous creature too prone to do what Papa or James wish of me, but I do yearn for more," I say. "If I were at liberty to choose my own fate, this would not be it." I turn to face Nate. "Please do not be cross with me. I do so hate our arguments. They are so very taxing."

Nate's long strides carry him back to me. His work-roughened hands find my face as he kisses me repeatedly between whispered apologies. "I'm sorry. I'm sorry. Never leave me. I love you. I love you. I love you."

Haunting, Present Day
Meredith

"I DO NOT BELIEVE I want to tell you any more at present." I'm suddenly aware I've closed the book on that memory and am once again standing in the circular library in my mind. I know where the memory leads. I guess Mercy didn't want to share the details of her beach make-out session, which I get. I'm not into kissing and telling either. What's private should stay private. Especially since she wasn't supposed to be seeing Nate.

"Do you wish to find another memory to explore?" Catalina asks.

"No."

Just like with the deepening and visualization, Catalina leads me through the process of awakening from a hypnotic state. I open my eyes, back in the present, and stare at the ceiling for a moment, trying to adjust to what I've seen and heard and even what was left unspoken. "Mercy has her secrets," I say, barely recognizing my own voice. "She didn't want to share everything."

Catalina tears off a sheet of paper and pops out a cassette tape from a mini recorder. "You should write what you saw that she didn't want to share." She comes around the desk to hand the page of notes and tape recording of the session to me. "Usually, more insight comes to you once you write your own impressions of the sessions." She glances toward where Jay and Nathan are sitting. "Are you ready, Nathan?"

"I think so." Nathan gets to his feet and swaps places with me on the recliner. Catalina leads him through the same breathing, deepening, and visualization techniques she used on me. My heart pounds as she asks the first question.

"What year is it?"

"1888." Nathan answers like the information is coming from deep inside.

"Can you tell me your name?"

"Nate Thatcher."

"What are you doing now, Nate?"

"Serving. I got stuck with drinks. I hate servin' at the hotel galas. I'd rather be stuck washing up in the kitchen."

"Why don't you like serving at the galas?" Catalina asks.

"Because it shows the difference in our stations. It's easy enough to pretend we're the same when we're walkin' along the shore or talkin' on the Widow's Walk but here I'm just another servant and she's the boss's daughter."

"Who is she?"

He acts like he's unwilling to answer despite his earlier talkativeness, but finally says, "Mercy."

"Can you tell us more about you and Mercy, Nate?"

There's another long pause like he's considering the question. "Yes, but don't be goin' and tellin' her what I say 'bout her."

"I won't. I promise," Catalina says. "Please, whenever you're ready, Nate."

He sighs. "I'm ready."

Haunting, 1888
Nate Thatcher

WHOEVER THOUGHT to put red and yellow together in a ball gown for Mercy was not thinkin' with their head. They shoulda picked one color or the other but not both. She looks like that circus trapeze girl me and the mates saw in Denver on our last day off before the season started.

"Wine, Madame?" I hold the tray out to Mercy and try to affect a posh accent instead of my usual rough-around-the-edges one. I hold my nose up in the air for good measure. Posh people have been lookin' down their noses at me my whole life. I might as well return the favor —even if just for a night.

Mercy laughs. "Thank you, kind sir."

"Are ya tired out yet from all that twirling and whirling with Mr. Whoever-Is-Next on your dance card?" I ask.

"You didn't drop your g's. Fantastic." She brushes up against me on purpose. I about drop my tray full of wine glasses but recover before I make a mess of the dance floor and the night.

"I've been practicin'." I exaggerate the Irish brogue that still creeps in no matter how long I've been away from the Old Country. I came to work in America, and work I found. I also found the great class divide is alive and well even across an ocean. Instead of living the American Dream in the land of opportunity, I receive constant reminders of why I'm good enough. Mercy, bless her, looks beyond the "immigrant" and "poor" labels to see the person beneath. Not all from her social circle do—or will. Sometimes I think we're fooling ourselves thinking what we have is more than a flirtation. Society won't welcome me, and all doors will be shut to her if she does marry me. I could die tomorrow, and my tombstone will read "Nathaniel Thatcher: Irish Immigrant" instead of "Nathaniel Thatcher: Chased The American Dream." I pity shortsighted people. I'm glad Mercy isn't one of those.

Mercy motions at James Piper, banker and railroad heir, as he twirls Miss Marianne Mills aroun' the floor. I dislike the man, but I won't deny he can cut an impressive rug on the dance floor. "James tried to fill my card, but I needed to leave some spots open. I am not his property."

"Does he know that?" I ask.

Mercy laughs. The sound is music to my ears. If I could grab her hand and run off this instant with no one stoppin' us, I would.

"Jilt him," I say instead. "Go on and cause a scandal. It will be the talk of the hotel for months, but talk always dies down if you give it time. No one will remember you or me or him in ten years or less. We'll just be another story. Just another tale to tell from a time best forgotten."

"I cannot jilt James." Her eyes widen in fear at the thought.

"Why not?"

"Because Papa would be livid. He would disown me for going against his wishes. Then where would I be with no money or home?" Her hand brushes against mine. "Where would we be? I have never worked a day in my life, Nate. As romantic as elopement sounds, it is not practical in the least bit. Even you have got to know that."

"Even if it is impractical, it would make you much happier." I run a finger along the gobs of jewels around her neck she calls a trinket.

"If ya sold even one jewel from this trinket, we could live like kings in the Irish District of New York. I got friends that work the rails still. They'd never rat us out to your pops or James. We could be free just to be you and me. No family, no class system, just us."

"As tempting as that sounds, I cannot leave Haunting. It is my home. It always has been and always will be." Mercy removes my hand from her neck lest someone think I'm bein' cheeky.

"We can make anywhere a home as long as we're together," I insist. "Would ya really miss all this?" I motion around the ballroom. "All this fuss and muss over something as silly as a little dancin'?" I squeeze her hand before droppin' it when James looks our way. "You know I can't give ya all this. I can't give you parties and ball gowns and fancy food. Life will be simple with me, but we'd be happy. I know it. Ya know it too, don't ya?"

"Mercy, dearest, stop fraternizing with the help and come dance the waltz!" James Piper sweeps over like the trussed-up peacock he is and ushers her away from me. Mercy looks over her shoulder at me and mouths "I'm sorry, Nate" as they take their places as the center of attention she deserves to be. The music starts and—for a time—she's lost to me in a world I cannot follow.

"No MORE." Nathan's voice holds Nate Thatcher's lilt still even though I can tell he's pulling himself out of the memory. "I don't want to talk on it no more."

Catalina shuffles papers on her desk before taking Nathan through the same steps as me to awaken him from the hypnotic state.

He opens his eyes, blinking several times. "I don't think it ended well for them. I mean, I know we figured that, but now—being back there—I'm pretty certain that it didn't end well for them."

"Write your impressions." Catalina hands Nathan her notes and the tape of the session. "It helps solidify everything you've learned from the session."

"Can we go now?" Jay looks up from his phone. At least he's had social media and games to keep him company while we've had our sessions. I don't want to say anything out loud, because I know he doesn't believe in the metaphysical to begin with, but my brief glimpse of James Piper in the past is enough to convince me that the triangle that Mercy found herself in is alive and well in the present day. That's one soul-pattern I'm repeating.

We gather up our stuff and trail Catalina back to the front office. I wave Nathan's attempt to pay away by insisting on charging both sessions to my dad's Gold Card. "Don't worry about this," I say. "With a name like Open Closed Doors, he'll think it's a hardware store."

No one talks as we make the short trek back to the car, climb in, and buckle up. My phone beeps letting me know I have a text message. I glance down at the screen. It's from Nathan in the back seat.

Nathan: *Notes 2gether 2nite?*

Me: *My rm @ 8. No J.*

Nathan: *Break dorm visit rule?*

Me: *Important enough 2.*

"Well, that was a big waste of all our time," Jay complains as he starts the car. "I hope you don't expect me to come here again, Mer."

"No. No, of course not," I say. I have years of practice of being able to answer while only half-listening. Now is one of those times. I clutch my cell phone tighter, my mind already focusing on 8 p.m. Yes, we'll be breaking Dad's after-hours dorm visitation rule, but it will be worth it. If push comes to shove, I'm sure I can get both of us off any academic probation. I need to discuss what we discovered today. If that means bending the rules a little bit, so be it.

Chapter 21

"Hey, wow, jeans," Nathan teases when I answer his knock on my dorm door, wearing jeans and a t-shirt instead of my usual dressier school clothes Dad insists on. "Does your dad make you wear skirts and dresses to class to uphold the family image?"

"Dad says a good girl from a good family needs to dress the part." I motion for him to take a seat on the bed or at my desk as I close the door behind him. He chooses the desk, and I take up residence on my bed, my bare feet dangling over the edge. The part of me that listens to Dad and Jay knows I should have waited until morning to discuss this with Nathan. Inviting a boy to my room alone after dorm visitation hours is a huge no-no, but I did it anyway. The need to compare notes and discuss what we experienced this afternoon at Open Closed Doors supersedes following the rules. I can't be the good girl every second of my life. It's exhausting. I need to remember to be me.

"So, what did you think about this afternoon?" Nathan pushes both hands through his hair, a characteristic I have noticed signals his emotions are on edge. "Crazy how real it was, right? I really felt like I was at that party."

"It was super intense," I agree. "It was like we *were* Mercy and Nate again, even if just for a little while, under hypnosis."

"I've read the soul is like a multifaceted gem," Nathan says. "Any time you turn it, it can reveal a new facet. Who knows how many pieces make up who we are? I bet there's a deeper connection than just Mercy and Nate if we keep looking." He digs a notebook and pen out of his backpack to write notes. "I told Jay I was going to the library for a late study session. He seemed to buy it."

"As long as we keep any excuses plausible and don't act like we're creeping around, Jay will buy it."

"We?" Nathan raises both dark eyebrows at me. "I didn't know there was a 'we' now. When did that happen?"

I wave a hand. Words stick in my throat. I'm not sure I should answer his question or if there's even an answer to give. We've talked about being in this together. After reliving moments in Nate and Mercy's lives this afternoon, the "in it together" idea seems all the more appropriate. There's a "we," even if it's not quite the "you and me" relationship Nathan wants. There's no denying that we have a connection. We have a responsibility to figure out Nate and Mercy's story together.

"Have you written any impressions down like Catalina asked us to?" I change the subject instead of answering if there was a "we" or not.

Nathan shakes his head. "I thought we should do it together. It will make it easier to discuss, don't you think? I mean, I'd rather just get it all out right now instead of holding anything back. The more we know, the clearer the whole picture becomes."

I find some paper and a pen of my own. "How should we do this?" I ask. "Bullet points? Paragraphs? A story?"

"It's not a test," Nathan says. "Why don't we just write and see what happens. Then we can compare notes. What I think will be really interesting is seeing how they—or we through their filter—each view different events."

I chew on the tip of my pen. "It won't differ much from today. The triangle pattern is already repeating itself. I saw that one loud and clear."

Nathan holds his pen over his open notebook. "You ready?"

I laugh. "Not really, but let's get this over with."

I write *THOUGHTS ON MERCY* at the top of my page and make a list.

- *Don't know if born in Haunting, but raised here. Dad ran Paradise Shores Hotel.*
- *Must have met Nate at the hotel. He worked there. Nate from wrong side of the tracks so couldn't be together. She had to "stick to her own kind."*
- *Engaged? Dating? James Piper—rich guy from her social circle obsessed with keeping up appearances.*
- *In love with Nate. Saw him when possible. He liked talking about their future together, but she never committed to anything because it went against "what they expected" of her.*
- *Something bad happened to her, him, or both. If there were a happy ending, there wouldn't be any need to correct the mistakes of the past now.*

"You finished?" I ask Nathan once he puts down his pen.

"Yeah," he says. "What did you get?"

"Just facts really," I say. "Nothing earth-shattering or insightful. I thought I'd just get the basics out first and then maybe expand from there into thoughts and feelings." I read off my list. "How about you? What did you get?"

"Similar to yours," Nathan says. "I listed a bunch of facts. Irish, worked the railroad before joining the Paradise Shores kitchen staff, in love with Mercy, upset she wouldn't run off with him, they had an epic fight, something bad happened."

"Nate wanted Mercy to elope?" I glance down at my paper to see if I wrote that too but skipped it in the read-through. I know it's true, even though it's not on my list. "Do you think it didn't happen?"

"If they had a happy ending, we wouldn't be making lists about people who died over a hundred years ago or have two psychic strangers tell us we need to 'correct' the mistakes of the past." Nathan scribbles something onto his paper.

"What did you write?" I ask.

"Jealous of Mercy's boyfriend." He grins. "Before you say anything, I know, I know. It's something I need to work on this time around too. See? Another pattern repeating itself."

"Maybe that's the biggest lesson of all to take from all this self-discovery," I say. "We need to recognize the soul-patterns and work to fix them. Some of Mercy's, which I've picked up, are thinking with her head instead of her heart and doing what other people expect instead of what she wants."

"Like dating Jay?" Nathan's voice holds the same edge of jealousy that's easy to spot in Jay's tone whenever Nathan is mentioned.

"Don't even get me started on the whole dating-Jay thing," I warn. "When we're alone, he's not the jerk you seem to think he is. He's jealous, too, and scared. Cut him some slack, will ya?"

"But if we're looking for patterns to fix or change, that's the biggest one of all." Nathan leans forward in his chair, blue eyes intense. "You're repeating Mercy and James. He was who society deemed 'appropriate,' so she tolerated him just like you tolerate Jay."

"Don't act like you know my feelings." I close my notebook and contemplate throwing it at him before changing my mind and throwing it on the floor instead. It still makes a satisfying slapping sound, which lessens some of my building anger. "I don't know how Mercy felt about James, but I know I don't just tolerate Jay. There's a goodness in him. A kindness. He's helped me through some of the roughest times of my life."

"So, you think you owe him something?" Nathan isn't letting go of his Nate-colored-glasses version of my life. "I don't care who he is or what he's done in the past. Just from what I've seen now, Meredith, I think you'd be happier without him."

"You think I'd be happier with you, you mean?" I accuse. "Typical male. Thinking all the problems of the world can be fixed by jumping from one guy to another. If you were in Jay's place, you wouldn't be pushing me to break it off. If you were in Jay's place, you'd be telling me to stay as far away from you as possible."

"If I were in Jay's place, I wouldn't treat you like he does."

"You haven't known me that long. What gives you the right to say something like that?"

"It wouldn't matter if we knew each other for two years, two weeks, or two days, Meredith, because *our souls* recognize each other. You can try to rationalize it and explain it away with science and facts and figures, but it's true. You know it's true."

Nathan's suddenly kneeling in front of me. He puts his hands on either side of my face and looks up at me with such an earnest—such a Nate—expression that my body sways toward him. I can't help it. It feels like an invisible cord is pulling me.

"You feel it. I know you feel it," Nathan whispers. "If you don't, what's the point of remembering?"

"I feel it," I murmur. "I feel it. Oh, Nathan, what are we going to do?"

A shock of images floods my mind as our lips meet. Mercy and Nate laughing as they dance in the rain to music only they can hear. Nate stealing a kiss behind the safety of Mercy's parasol. Mercy and Nate lounging in each other's arms in a hotel-owned sailboat with no destination in mind—just content to be together. There's a calmness —a sureness—when they're together that I hope to find someday. But with who?

Would that sureness be with Nathan or Jay?

I don't remember when we stop kissing and just lie side by side on my bed, Nathan's arms around me and my head resting on his chest. I close my eyes and listen to his deep, even breathing. I know I should feel guilty a million times over for a million different things—breaking curfew rules, kissing someone else while committed to Jay—but none of that seems to bother me while I'm wrapped in Nathan's arms.

"I could stay like this forever," I murmur.

"You won't hear any arguments from me," Nathan says. "Meredith, I will probably spoil everything; I do that with the whole open-mouth, insert-foot thing, but we need to talk about this. We need to talk about us."

I squeeze my eyes shut tight, wanting to avoid any discussions for as long as possible. "Can't we just let it go for a while? Why do we always have to talk right away?" I sit up and put some space between us. "I don't want to talk. Just let it be."

Nathan sits up too. "We're running in circles, Meredith. Maybe not you and me for all that long, but Nate and Mercy were, and we're repeating their mistakes. Do you want to just let that be?"

"No, but that's not something we can do alone. We need to go back to Open Closed Doors. I don't know about you, but I have more questions now than when we started."

Nathan reaches for my hand, but I pull away. "Don't do this, Meredith." His voice is low, almost coaxing, but I do my best to ignore the pleading. "Don't go back into your box after you've tasted freedom."

"Let me make my own decisions, Nathan. That's part of what freedom is." I stand and move to the door before opening it. I stick my head out to check if the hall is all clear. I'm surprised more people don't sneak around after curfew. Maybe the wrath of Dad is more powerful than I think.

"So, what now?" Nathan asks as he slips into the hallway undetected.

"You call Catalina and set up appointments," I decide. "Jay already said he wants nothing more to do with this, so asking him to come along or borrowing his car to get downtown is out. We must go to plan B."

"What's plan B?"

Plan B is only half-formed in my head as the words come out: "I'll ask my dad to loan us his car."

"Enter," Dad's deep voice calls as I knock on his office door the next morning after breakfast. He's never been in the running for Father of the Year, but at least when Mom was alive, he attempted to eat meals with me, as opposed to now.

"Hey, Dad, I have a question to ask you." I slip into the office and shut the door behind me. "It won't take very long. Do you got a sec?"

He looks up from his mountain of paperwork when he notices it's me and not just some random person asking for a favor. "Meredith, shouldn't you be in class?"

"My first class doesn't start until nine." I hold my hands behind my back, feeling like I'm about to be assigned detention instead of having a talk with my father.

Dad pulls off his reading glasses and studies me as if I'm a stranger, and I suppose I am. He has taken little interest in me besides my grades and who I'm dating since Mom died. "In that case, what can I do for you?"

"I need a car or, well, at the very least, to borrow yours."

"What about Jay? He doesn't mind playing chauffeur for you."

I should have known Dad wouldn't roll over so easily. I may be his only child, but I can't just walk in, ask for car keys without an explanation, and expect to get them. Dad calling Jay my chauffeur makes me wonder how much of Jay's car-borrowing compliance is Dad pulling strings behind the scenes. I always considered Dad relatively hands off—too focused on running the school to care what I did—but has he been pulling the strings behind the scenes the whole time? Has he been telling Jay to keep watch so he doesn't have to? Was that the real reason he wanted us together?

"Jay's busy with practice. He can't help out today." The lie may be the truth considering how Jay lives to ski. "Please, Dad? It's important school-related stuff. Nathan and I have a living history project due soon. We need to research a store downtown." I left out the part that Ritzi is also in our group but not going on our "research" trip. He could figure that out for himself if he cared to. "Jay's not interested in going," I add. "I dragged him along on the first trip. All he did was complain. I kind of want to avoid that this time."

"How are things with you and Jay?" Dad fishes his Corvette keys out of his pocket and swings them back and forth on his finger like a pendulum. I get the impression that whether I get those keys or not depends on my answer to his me-and-Jay question.

I think back to the night on the Widow's Walk. If things were always that simple and Jay always that vulnerable, I would have no problem saying great. But they're not always that simple, and Jay's not always that vulnerable. Instead of trying to figure everything out while staring down Dad, I push it aside like everything else in my life. "Things are like they always are with Jay, Dad," I say instead. "Nothing new to report. If there is, you'd be the first to know."

"When do you need the car?"

I'm so close to accomplishing my goal. I reach for the keys but pull my hand back. I can't seem too eager. "I don't know yet. I need to get with my group and figure out when we're going downtown. Maybe you can just give me the spare key?"

"I saw a $100 charge on my Gold Card for an Open Closed Doors in town." Dad hands over a wad of cash for what I assume is gas money and the spare key to his Corvette. "Would that be part of this Colorado History project as well?"

"It's a new living history experience." I'm surprised at how easily the lies continue to come. "It's a little pricey because there's so much there. It's kind of like the Haunting version of Disney World. I bought some stuff at the gift shops to use as props in our presentation. I know I should have asked first, but since it's for school, I didn't think you'd mind. Maybe you can write it off on your taxes as a business expense since it's school-related?"

"Just make sure you make an A on this project." Dad leans forward and pats my cheek like I'm six instead of sixteen. "No daughter of mine will set a bad example."

"Yes, sir." I turn to leave. I hesitate at the door, my hand hovering over the knob. "Is there anything else, Dad?"

"Be nice to Jay," Dad says. "He's just the sort of young man I think you can have a nice, comfortable life with."

I bite down hard on my bottom lip until I taste blood. Well, if we're looking for patterns, here's another staring us right in the face. Mercy's dad pushed her to be with James. My dad is doing the same with Jay. "Yes, Dad, I'll do my best," I whisper before retreating into the hallway.

Once I'm in the safety of the empty hall, I dig out my cell phone to text Nathan. *Mission accomplished. Car keys mine. When appt?*

I don't have to wait long before a response flashes across my screen: *Fri. 5. Meet u @ ur rm.*

The week passes far too fast. The closer Friday gets, the more nervous I feel. It's not that I'm against understanding the full picture of Nate and Mercy's story; it's just I'm afraid of the answers we'll find when we do explore all aspects of their lives. It's a lot to take in. She became me. Her mistakes and choices are *my* mistakes and choices; that personal tie and connection to the story makes it impossible for me to stay neutral.

I look up from throwing some last-minute things into my purse on Friday afternoon when I hear a tentative knock on my door. I wiggle my feet into my shoes and hurry to answer the door. It's not Nathan on the other side of the door, though. It's Ritzi. And she's been crying.

"Ritzi! What's wrong?"

"Can I come in?" Ritzi dabs at her already-streaky makeup. "I need to talk to someone, and you're the first person I thought of."

I usher her inside and close the door after her. We both sit on my bed. I've never really had a girlfriend before, so I'm not sure what to do in this situation. I decide just to sit and wait until Ritzi feels ready to talk.

"Oh, I've interrupted something." Her eyes fill with tears again when she notices my purse next to the door, and that I'm still dressed in my fancier school clothes versus already changed into sweats and a t-shirt. "You're getting ready to go somewhere. Don't mind me. It's not a big deal. I'm probably being dumb anyway. Reading too much into things as usual. That's what I do, you know."

"Reading too much into what?" I lay my hand on top of hers to show support. "Ritzi, just tell me what happened. I'm your friend, remember? I'm here to help."

"Well, I was texting Nathan, you know, and I thought we had something going or, at least were building up to something."

"Nathan?" That makes me sit up and take notice. "My Nathan? I —I mean Nathan from history class? That Nathan?"

Ritzi nods. "Yeah. Remember when I asked you about him before because you guys are always hanging out? Well, I scored his number after class last week, and we've been texting. Again, it's probably me reading too much into things. I bet I read between the lines or saw what I wanted to see instead of what was there. I just, well, I just really like him, you know? It's hard when you think things are going one way, and then you get completed ghosted."

"Ghosted?" I'm only a little familiar with the term. I think she means Nathan stopped texting her back, which would be dumb since he sees her in class and on campus every day. You can't just cut ties with someone you see in person every day. "Can I, uh, see the texts? It might give me a better idea of what's going on," I add, so it doesn't seem like I just want to snoop around her phone or be up in her private business.

Ritzi hands over her phone. "If you think it will help."

I skim through the text message chain between Nathan and her. Ritzi is very flirty with a lot of emojis. I'm relieved to see Nathan is polite but not encouraging. Whatever Ritzi thought or hoped was happening, Nathan is innocent of leading her on.

"Nathan is a good guy, Ritzi." I hand her phone back to her. "I think there's been some sort of mix-up. Just talk to him. I'm sure he'll be more than happy to clear up any confusion."

"Do you really think so?"

"I know so." I get up to answer a second knock on my door. I forget until my hand is on the knob that I'm expecting Nathan. The only thing that can be remotely on the same level of awkward as me, Jay, and Nathan together in the same room is me, Ritzi, and Nathan together in the same room.

Nathan looks back and forth between Ritzi and me. "Hey, Ritzi, I didn't know you'd be here."

"I live right next door," she says. "I didn't know you planned to stop by either."

"Meredith and I have an appointment downtown." He shoots me a look that says "get us out of here as fast as you can."

"Um, hey, Ritzi, is it okay if we pick this up later?" I ask. "I don't want to miss the appointment."

She frowns, looking disappointed, but agrees anyway. "Sure, if you have to. Have fun without me."

I'm not sure what to say to that, so I grab my purse and wait for Nathan and Ritzi in the hall. When they're both out of the room, I lock up, Ritzi heads back to her room, and Nathan and I head for the staircase.

"*What* was that all about?" he asks as we walk through the parking lot to Dad's waiting Corvette.

"Remember when I said she likes you?" I stop in front of Dad's car and dig the key out of my purse, then unlock the doors and climb in. I'm not super comfortable driving, but I doubt Dad would want Nathan behind the wheel of his four-wheeled baby.

Nathan squints as he tries to recall the memory. "Vaguely."

"Well, that's what that was all about." I wave a hand to organize my thoughts. "She thought you were ghosting her when you didn't answer her texts. I tried to talk her down from the ledge. You showing up may have made it worse." I don't want to say the next words. I dread the answer, though I have no right to feel nervous or jealous over an answer from a boy who I have no claim over. He is not mine, no matter what I slipped up and said in my room. "Is there anything going on with you two?"

Nathan laughs, but I still need to hear the words. I still need to hear him deny that there's anything going on. It's the only way this ache in my heart will stop. "Is there anything going on with Ritzi and me?" He fiddles with his seatbelt as I pull out of the parking lot and head toward downtown.

"I didn't know it was such a hard question to answer." There's an edge to my voice—the same chilliness I've heard in both Jay's and Nathan's voices. Now I'm jealous. We might as well form a club.

"It's easy to answer," he says. "It's the easiest thing in the world for me to say—at least on my part. There's nothing going on between Ritzi and me. She's cool and all, but the only one I want anything going on with is you, Meredith." He rests a hand on my knee as I drive. "You've always been the only one I want."

I practically yank Nathan's arm out of its socket when my feet stall out on the steps of Open Closed Doors. He stops and looks over at me.

"What's wrong?" he asks. "We're here now. You just need to put one foot in front of the other. You can do it, Meredith. Trust me, if I can, you can."

I stare up at the shop sign, willing my uncooperative feet to move. They don't listen. It's like I've suddenly grown roots and will just stand outside and stare forever. "I'm afraid of what we will find out. I don't want to know how she died." I shudder. "I don't want to know how either of them died. Why can't we just leave it alone? Why can't we just agree that we're us now and leave the past in the past?"

"Because it's affecting our present." Nathan squeezes my hand. "Maybe we've been going around in these same patterns for even longer than that. I don't know." He squeezes my hand again to show support. "All I know is tough choices have tough answers. Don't forget we're in this together, remember? I don't think Nate could stop what happened to Mercy with the whole her dying thing, but I won't let history repeat itself. I promise. Now, let's go inside, okay? We can do this. You're stronger than your fear."

The jolt of energy that passes through me as Nathan's fingers tighten around mine gives me just the amount of courage I need to walk through the door to find answers to the past. He's right. I *am* stronger than my fear. We both are. No matter what happened to Mercy and Nate, we can face it and learn from it. Even in the darkness, there is light.

"Welcome back." Catalina looks up from the reception desk when we enter. Today her hair is bright red with purple streaks.

"Remember," Nathan whispers as we follow Catalina to the back room, "Nate and Mercy have a story to tell. We owe it to them and to us to listen."

"You go first this time," I whisper back. Nathan squeezes both of my hands before taking his place on the recliner. I don't know why I'm dreading this session so much, but the queasy feeling in the pit of my stomach only intensifies as Catalina leads Nathan through the past-life regression breathing, deepening, and visualization techniques. Why am I so scared? What secrets is Mercy hiding deep in my past?

Haunting, 1888
Nate Thatcher

At least Mercy has class enough not to mention the flowers now overflowin' in her arms were yesterday's centerpieces. I scooped them up before the maids got to them. It seemed a shame to throw 'em out.

"What's the occasion?" She looks up at me with that smile of hers that could rival the sun for warmth.

"An anniversary of sorts," I say. "Three years and two months ago

I first saw ya, though it took three more months for me to buck up enough courage to say 'how do ya do.' Do you remember?" I watch as she buries her nose in the flowers. I feel a swell of pride knowin' that I gave those to her. I did. Not James, not any of those other swells hangin' around. Me.

"I remember you dropped a tray full of silverware," Mercy says. "James thought you were incompetent and asked Papa why he hired a clumsy 'mick.'"

"Water off the back." I dismiss the slur. James can call me whatever he pleases. I plan to get the last laugh. "With you, at least I didn't stay tongue-tied forever."

"Mm. I am glad. Life would be boring without you." She accepts my arm when I offer. She's doin' a bang-up job of holdin' on with one hand and balancin' the flowers with the other. "Sometimes being with you, Nate, seems *too* perfect." Mercy's face clouds as we stroll. "I wonder if it will last. Perfection rarely does."

"And when was the last time ya saw perfection?" I try to keep my voice light.

"Whenever I am with you." Her hand tightens on my arm as if to make sure I'm real. Say what you will about social classes, but I see the real Mercy, and that, I am sure, is more important to her than any fancy party or frilly dress.

"I am far from perfect."

"Oh, don't be silly." Mercy laughs—the sound as perfect as music. "I know no one is perfect, but this time with you feels like perfection, Nate. You do not care about society or what color my latest ball gown is. You do not care for news of the stock market or what the coal industry is up to. I like that, Nate. You are uncomplicated. I enjoy the simplicity. You make my life feel simple when we are together."

"You know I want little in this wide world, Mercy, besides your happiness," I confess. "The only other thing I want is the one thing you keep denyin' me. I wish ya'd agree to marry me. Just one little yes, Mercy. Is it so very hard to say yes?"

She purses her lips in the way I know means I done spoiled a promisin' afternoon. "You know it is not as simple as just saying yes, Nate," she reminds me. "I wish it was. I wish Papa allowed me to choose for myself. There is nothing I would love more than an uncomplicated life, but the second I walk through those hotel doors, my life is not my own. There are society's rules and consequences to consider and James and Papa's opinions, not to mention—"

"James Piper is a cowardly, stuff-shirt peacock hidin' behind his money an' manners and doesn't deserve to breathe the same air as you, Mercy, let alone have your loyalty!"

She turns her head, and her face shows shock and disappointment at my outburst. "Like it or not, Nate, James is who Papa wishes me to marry. I cannot go against that any more than you can go against your station in life. Please do not make me regret coming to meet you this afternoon. Please, can we just go back to before when all we needed to worry about was the sun shining and your arm on mine?"

"We already know your father's wishes and your wishes are at odds, Mercy." I'm unwilling and unable to let the subject go. "When are ya gonna stand up for yourself and do what makes you *happy* instead of what ev'ryone *expects*?"

"I don't know if I can, Nate." Mercy's face has gone as white as the hotel sheets. If I didn't know better, I'd say she was about to faint clean away. "It is too trying. Please, don't ask me again."

"So, you're tellin' me, you're willin' to give up what we have—what we mean to each other—just to stay off the front page of the society gossip rags?"

"If I have to." She bites her bottom lip. "Are you through with this line of questioning, Nate? If so, I should return before Papa and James worry."

"If you are willin' to give up everything we have just to stay out of the papers, then maybe what we have here is not as special as I thought. You're so concerned with what James and your pa and society think of you, you can't see how much your choice is killin' me. I'm *dying*, Mercy."

"Don't lie," she whispers. "You won't die without me, Nate. No one should have that sort of power over you."

I tap my chest with a fist. "If you feel even half for me of what I feel for you, your heart would be breakin' right now too. Are you so cold, so careless of others' emotions, that you'd walk away instead of facing what sort of havoc your choices cause others? We could have a good life, Mercy. Poor, yes, but good none the less. Tell me, what's so wrong with that?"

"Nothing's wrong with that. It's just not what I'm meant for, Nate." She dips her head to hide her face behind a curtain of blonde curls. "I'm sorry. I wish there were more than one choice for me, but there's not. There's only one, and it's not with you."

I pull my arm away and leave her without so much as a backward glance. I hear her cryin', which shatters my heart even more, but I can't look back. I can't. If I do, I'll just keep playin' this game. She's made her choice. It's him and society. Not me. I realize now it was never going to be me. I can't keep hangin' around trying to change her mind. It's already been made.

Chapter 25

Haunting, Present Day
Meredith

"Intense," Nathan says once he's back again in the present. He sits up straight and turns to find me. "Do you think she changed her mind? Do you think they ran off together like Nate wanted?"

I shrug, never feeling more helpless. "I wish I knew."

"Perhaps you'll find out today." Catalina motions for me to take my place on the recliner.

With a heavy heart, I trade places with Nathan.

Haunting, 1888
Mercy Stone

DESPITE ANY FAULTS he may have, James always has been—and always will be—an excellent dancer. He makes me feel safe, relaxed, and secure on the dance floor as he leads us about in a waltz. He is always confident but never demanding. I wish he took some of his charms on the dance floor into his everyday existence. I am apt to agree to just about anything after a waltz, which James fully knows.

"May I have a word with you in private, Mercy?" he requests once the music stops and the polite applause has died.

"Naturally, James." I follow him through the concealed door to the veranda off the grand ballroom. The hyacinth is in bloom, lending its sweet scent to the air. What I would not give for just a quiet moment to enjoy the fresh air and flowers, but James is not known for admiring nature. From experience, when James says he wishes a word, he will do quite a bit of talking. I will not enjoy a quiet evening on the veranda tonight.

"Let me start off by saying you know I have admired you for quite some time, Mercy," James begins without preamble. He does not even comment on my appearance or the loveliness of the night, which is his usual standard opening when requesting a word in private. "Even when you were in pigtails and short skirts, I knew you would grow into the fine woman you have become."

"Thank you, James." Short answers and pleasantries are all that is required to hold up my end of the interview.

He turns to face me. His face, normally flushed with life, looks pale in the moonlight. The glint in his eyes sends a ripple of fear through me. Though I know James is too keen on society's opinion to act untoward me, perhaps I have misjudged him and this interview. It is too late now to call it off, though. We are alone, and I need to do my best to deal with whatever may come my way.

"Thank you, James."

He seizes my hand, his own clammy with sweat. "You have become a fine woman, Mercy. It will come as no surprise, I am sure, when I tell you how very much I admire you and how well I believe we suit." He rubs his free hand down the side of his trousers. "We *do* suit, don't we, Mercy?"

"Papa believes so," I say.

"And what do you believe, little one?" His voice is half-teasing, his tone showing he already believes himself assured of his victory. I imagine I could tell him to go jump in the lake and still somehow come out engaged at the end of the night.

"I believe you have all the qualities I should want in a husband, James." I keep my voice slow and measured.

"*Should* want?" He catches my less-than-fawning choice of words. "Naturally, any woman *should* want the security I can provide, but what do *you* want, Mercy? Truly, do not toy with me. You know full well why I requested an audience here with you tonight."

"I want to be sure," I say. "I want to be sure what you propose is right."

"Perhaps a trial engagement, then?" James suggests. "It will give us a chance to know each other in a more intimate setting without the tricky hassle of a broken engagement if we part ways at a future date." He touches my cheek. "You can wear the ring on your right hand as a promise to me and, at the End of Season Ball, you can decide whether you wish to make it a more permanent arrangement." James's smile is coaxing, allowing me to believe he has only good intentions at heart. "Is that acceptable to you, little one?"

"Yes, James," I hear my own voice responding, while my heart aches for the pain my answer shall cause Nate.

Haunting, Present Day
Meredith

I LAY STARING at the ceiling long after Catalina brings me through the steps of returning to full consciousness. No matter how I look at it, what Nathan has been insisting all along is true. I *am* repeating the patterns of the past. I am. But how do I stop the cycle? Mercy buckled under the pressure. Will I do the same thing?

"How are you feeling?" Nathan asks when my staring at the ceiling lasts a little too long to get away with answering that I'm fine. "Are you feeling up to heading back to campus, or do I need to give you more time?"

I sit up in the recliner. "I'll be okay. Just give me a second."

I close my eyes and take several deep, steadying breaths to help ground me. I still feel a little off, like I'm half-stuck in the past. Nathan helps me off the recliner, and we pay Catalina and head outside. The fresh air hitting my face revives me more. I take another deep breath and look around like I'm seeing everything for the first time. My eyes fall on the gate to the graveyard. On a normal day, I'd avoid it like the plague, but today is far from normal.

"Nathan, let's stop."

He looks over his shoulder at me. "Stop where?"

I point at the gate. "The graveyard."

"Are you sure?" He grabs at my hand when I head in that direction. "Didn't you say you hate that place? Like, you can't stand being anywhere near it?"

"Yeah, usually, but today is different." I open the gate and step inside with Nathan close behind. "Maybe some of our answers are in here, and I've been too afraid to look until now."

We walk the crooked rows of tombstones together. I feel ghostly hands plucking at my clothes as a flood of voices whispers through my mind. Everyone wants to be heard and remembered. I don't have the mental strength to keep my guards and shields up today. I hear names and messages for loved ones. I should write them down, but I forgot to bring a notebook and pen.

I'm sorry, I tell them in my mind. *I can't help you today. I'll come back. I'll help you then. Tell me your stories then.*

"Meredith?" I look up when Nathan calls to me from one of the older sections of the graveyard. "Come look at this."

He's standing in front of two headstones with faded but very familiar names etched into them:

Mercy Stone 1867–1888

Nathaniel Thatcher 1865–1888

"They died the same year we went to in the regression."

Chapter 26

After the draining day at Open Closed Doors and our discovery in the cemetery, I'm happy to fall into a dreamless sleep. The next day is Saturday. Most Saturdays I'd hang out with Jay or read, but today I just want to pull the covers over my head and ignore everything. I know without having another dream or regression that Mercy Stone made the choice society deemed acceptable. She chose James. Pattern or no pattern, I don't see how it can end any different now. Jay is the easy choice for me, just like James was the easy choice for Mercy. It's easier for me to play along and stay in my gilded cage instead of setting myself free. The second I think I'm ready to bend the bars in my cage, I get overwhelmed and pull back. I can't do it. I just can't. It's too much to go against what Dad has taught me is the right thing to do. Maybe that makes me some sort of good girl robot, but I don't know how to be any different. I'm not strong enough—no matter what Nathan says.

My text message alert beeps. I check it. Speaking of Nathan. The text is from him. *Thinking of you* is all it says.

I ignore it. It's not my finest moment, but Nathan is so Nate-like

with his eternal optimism and "love conquers all" mentality that if I
tell him my thoughts are going in the maybe- Mercy-made-the right-
choice-by-picking-what-society-deemed-acceptable direction, he'll be
crushed. He'll think I'm giving up and not even attempting to fix the
past-life patterns or, as he deems them, mistakes. Whatever we have
going on between us is very new and fragile. We're friends for sure,
but we're also in a weird not-quite-a-couple limbo state. Does Nathan
expect the happy ending that Mercy and Nate didn't get? Am I brave
enough to break it off with Jay for him?

My text message alert beeps again.

Nathan: *We should talk. Coffee later?*

I'll only end up hurting him once he figures out I'm not the girl he
expects me to be.

Me: *I can't. Studying.*

Nathan: *On a Saturday?*

Me: *Big test on Monday. Sorry.*

The lie hurts almost as much as disappointing Nathan.

My phone rings. I check the screen. I expect it to be Nathan,
ready to talk me out of my supposed study plans, but it's Jay.

"Hey, babe. What's my favorite girl doing?" His voice sounds
distant like he's driving around some twisty mountain road.

"Waiting for you to call." One reason I stick to the safe path is
because I know what to expect. Jay always calls me every Saturday.
It's like clockwork. He's safe. He's steady. What's wrong with that?
"Let's go somewhere," I decide. "How soon can you pick me up?"

"I can be there in twenty," he says.

"Sounds perfect. I'll be ready."

Jay and I drive to Stone Lake. It's a favorite spot from when we were
first dating before things became so routine I forgot why I was dating
him. Now, it feels like forever since we've been up here.

"Remember when we used to come up here every weekend and

just sit by the water and talk?" I zip up my hoodie to protect myself from the cold breeze coming off the water. "It seems like so long ago. I don't even remember what we talked about."

"We talked about your mom." Jay wraps an arm around my shoulders and pulls me close as we walk. "You wanted to tell me everything about her. It was like if you got every memory out, they'd last twice as long with two people keeping them safe instead of just one. You don't talk about her anymore. Why not?"

"I guess I ran out of memories."

"Or maybe you found someone else to share them with."

"Don't say stuff like that, Jay. You know it's not true." I lean into him to block the wind—and to remind myself how protected I feel with Jay around. There's no doubt in my mind my safety and well-being would always come first if I took the path that leads to Jay.

"No, I don't know it's not true," he insists. "I've barely seen you alone in the last couple of weeks, and when I do, you're distracted. It's like you're dialing in your alone time with me. What am I supposed to think, Meredith? Tell me, 'cause I'd really like to know."

"All you need to think is I've had a lot on my mind." I look at the sky, watching the clouds drift by. "I'm distracted. It's nothing more than that. I'm sorry if you think I've been neglecting you. That wasn't my intention at all."

"Then what was your intention?"

I close my eyes and pinch the bridge of my nose with my thumb and index finger. "Are we going to do this now? Can't we just have a nice afternoon, Jay?"

"You're right. You're right," he agrees. "I wanted to make this a perfect afternoon for us, and now I'm screwing it all up."

We sit on the sandy steps leading to the lake swimming area. Jay brushes off the third step before taking off his jacket for us to sit on. We're silent, just sitting side by side watching the water lap at the shore before Jay speaks up again.

"Hey, do you really believe in that fix-the-mistakes-of-the-past-or-be-doomed-to-repeat-them-forever stuff?" he asks.

I stare at the water, remembering how many times Mercy and Nate ran off to a lake to be alone. Was this their lake? "Sometimes, I don't know what I believe anymore."

"'Cause I was doing some research into this James Piper guy that Psychic Granny said I looked like, and some things kind of matched up."

I sit up straighter, surprised at this news. "Jay! You looked into it yourself?"

Color floods his cheeks. "Yeah, um, it's not a big deal. I thought I'd check some old newspapers and stuff since he was supposed to be a big society guy around this area. I found out that, after his fiancée died, he never married. He was loyal, see? I get that. I would do the same thing if that were me instead of him. No one could ever replace you in my heart, Meredith." I open my mouth to say something, but Jay plows on before his words or courage can fail him. "I know we're young and we don't talk that much about love and all that, but I really can't imagine what my life would be like without you. I don't want to imagine what my life would be like without you, Mer."

"You never will." I squeeze his knee. "We were friends first, remember? That will never change."

"The thing is, I don't think just friends is enough for me. Not after what we've had for the last couple of years." He gulps down his fear and keeps talking. "I'm turning pro in May after graduation. I know that's a big decision and I should have asked what you thought first, but skiing is, like, my job. Going pro is like going from part-time to full-time." Jay holds his hand palm up toward me. I take it. "I didn't skip senior year because I didn't want to lose what we had, Mer. I still don't want to lose it."

"Friends first, remember?" My chest constricts. It feels like I'm losing him already. "Congrats. I know you'll be great on the pro circuit, Jay. With or without me cheering you on."

"But that's the point I'm trying to make and doing it badly." Jay brushes his windswept hair out of his face with his free hand and looks at me straight on for the first time since we got to the lake. "I don't want to ever be without you, Meredith. I don't know how. I mean, I know I had fourteen years before I met you and all, but they weren't the greatest. I like to think I didn't really live until your dad introduced us."

My free hand flutters to my heart. This is the real Jay. This is the reason he's my boyfriend—not because his parents are rich or my dad says he's from the right social circle. I date him because he cares for me. That goes a long way. I'm convinced Dad can't remember my birthday and wouldn't remember my full name if it wasn't printed on my student file, but Jay always remembers.

"Jay, I love that you're so sure about us, but I couldn't live with myself if you limited your future because of me," I say. "Just think about that, okay? Life outside of Haunting will be so exciting for you. It won't take you long to forget all about me."

"Why would you say something like that? I could never forget all about you," Jay insists. "Am I supposed to act like the last years have meant nothing to me? I can't do that, Mer. I just can't."

"What do you suggest?" The words come out a little breathy as a memory flashes through my mind of Mercy and James having a similar conversation on the veranda at the Paradise Shores Hotel. A talk where James proposed at the end of it. Is that what's happening now? Could Jay be proposing?

"Well, I know we're still young, and I totally don't expect you to say yes yet, but a maybe would be cool."

My heart thumps in my chest. He is. Oh, gosh, what am I going to say when he gets the words out, and I'm supposed to give an answer? Maybe I'm reading too much into things. What are the odds I have a memory of Mercy getting engaged to James right before Jay asks me practically the same thing?

"A maybe to what, Jay? You haven't asked me anything yet."

"Oh! Um, I was wondering if you'd want to marry me. Not now, but in a couple years after I've been on the pro circuit for a while. I got a ring. It doesn't have to be an engagement ring just yet. It can be a, you know, promise ring. I guess I should show it to you first before you make any sort of decision. It can take the place of the Claddagh ring I gave you before. You know, something a little more permanent. You can even wear it on your right hand for now like the Claddagh ring." He fumbles around in his pocket before producing a box with the biggest non–engagement ring diamond I've ever seen sitting inside.

Words from another time and place float back to me at the sight of Jay's gift. *You can wear the ring on your right hand as a sort of promise to me and, at the End of Season Ball, you can decide whether you wish to make it a more permanent arrangement.* Like Mercy, I find myself tired and more than a little overwhelmed with what society expects of me. *Rich girls don't marry poor boys.* That's what a girl told writer F. Scott Fitzgerald once. It stuck with him so much that he used it in *The Great Gatsby*. My dad would parrot the sentiment, I'm sure, if he ever guessed my mind and heart were a big jumbled mess. For him, there was only one choice, and I better make it. Or else.

"So, what do you say?" Jay looks so hopeful that I can't bust his heart into a million pieces.

But what about Nathan?

As much as I try to push my growing feelings for Nathan aside, they're still there, blooming. No matter how many times I tell myself Jay is the one I'm with, Jay is the one I want, my heart still asks, "What about Nathan?" Is it even possible to have feelings for two boys at once? Jay is safe and everything I should want. Nathan challenges me in ways I've never been challenged before. I know we're not living in the 1800s and society's rules aren't as strict as they were for Mercy and Nate, but can I really go against everything that's been drilled into me since an early age just on the off chance that a poor, scholarship student like Nathan might make me happy? I can't guarantee a rich sports star like Jay will make me happy either, but at least he's familiar and safe. I know what to expect. Too much of any potential relationship with Nathan seems to hinge on not falling into the same soul-patterns that we may or may not have been repeating for centuries. What if I choose neither? What if I focused on figuring out who *I* was solo instead of part of a relationship? Do I really always want to be examining myself and my relationship like that? Sure, it means soul growth, but at what price?

I shake my head. Like Mercy, I was raised to be pretty and do what others expected of me. Everything in me says I'm so much more than that, but it's still so hard to change. Instead, I make the same choice Mercy Stone made all those years ago when faced with the same decision. I might hate myself in the morning, and I know for sure Nathan will hate me in the morning, but I do it anyway. I take the easy way out.

I take off my Claddagh ring and hold out my right hand to Jay. "It's gorgeous, babe. I'd be proud to wear your promise ring."

Chapter
27

I jolt out of a dreamless sleep to someone pounding on my door. I sit up, confused. For a second, I almost call out for James before remembering where I'm at and using the right name—the modern name—instead.

"Jay, if this is supposed to be a head's up to someone pulling the fire alarm, tell the guys they won't catch anyone in the shower at this hour," I call. "All the sane people are asleep. You should be too."

"Meredith, why haven't you been answering my calls or texts?" Nathan's muffled voice asks. "Could you please open the door? We need to talk."

My heart jumps at the sound of his voice, no matter how much I tell myself it shouldn't. I have Jay's promise ring on my finger. I shouldn't have such a reaction to someone else.

"There's nothing to talk about," I call. "Go back to your room, Nathan."

"If you really believe we have nothing to talk about, Meredith, you're lying to more people than just yourself."

I slide out of bed, pad across the floor, and open the door a crack.

Nathan looks desperate. His dark hair is disheveled. He's also barefoot and wearing a faded high school track team t-shirt with flannel pajama pants. "It's past inter-dorm curfew," I say. "Do you want to get us both in trouble? Maybe even expelled?"

"I don't care about that," Nathan says. "It's not like curfew stopped us before. Or do you only break the rules when it's convenient for you?"

"That's not fair, Nathan, and you know it." We stare each other down before I relent. "Fine. What do you want to talk about?"

"You know what about!" Nathan shouts before I shush him by clamping a hand over his mouth and pulling him into my dorm room. "You know what about," he repeats quieter once we're inside with the door shut.

"Is this about Jay?" I ask. "I figured he couldn't resist saying something once we got back from Stone Lake."

Nathan looks confused. "What are you talking about?"

Relief floods through my entire body. I have some time before I have to crush him. Good. The more time I can buy, the better. "It's nothing. Don't worry about it. What are you talking about?"

"I'm talking about how we left Mercy and Nate's story unfinished," Nathan says. "I think we need to go back at least once more or we'll never know what we need to avoid this time around. It's like walking away from a puzzle with one piece left to put in place. We need to finish this journey, Meredith. Didn't Mrs. King at Psychic Square say Mercy and Nate weren't at peace? Maybe getting the whole story out will help them rest."

"A lot of ghosts around here are restless, Nathan." I try to dismiss his concern, even though the thought of Mercy and Nate with unfinished business or unable to move on hurts my heart. "They aren't the first and won't be the last."

"But they were us." He reaches for my hand, but I pull away. Hurt flashes across his face. Hurt I caused. Nathan takes a deep breath, seeming to recover from the disappointment. "Their issues are our issues, Meredith. If they can't move on, neither can we."

"We may have similar physical appearances and personality traits, but I think you're forgetting that we are our own people now." I move away from Nathan to sit on my unmade bed. "I'm glad we know about the soul-patterns. I'm glad we know what to look out for and avoid, but soul-patterns are patterns for a reason. It's not as easy as you think to break them."

"You just have to try a little harder." Nathan sits next to me and reaches for my left hand. This time I let him take it. I hide my right hand with Jay's ring under my pillow. "These memories, these connections, these dreams are like being given a second chance, Meredith. We screwed up before. We made the wrong choices. Now we have a second chance. Do you know how rare that is?"

"No, but I bet you're about to tell me."

"Don't brush this aside," Nathan warns. "It's not a joke. Have you ever felt restless? Have you felt like there was something left unsaid or undone in your life?"

"Of course I have," I say. "We've been over this already. I've always felt like there's something or someone missing. That feeling's gotten stronger since my mom died. It's like I'm searching. I just don't know for what."

"Exactly. You might think all the things you're searching for are related to the present, but I think I relate at least some of those missing pieces to Nate and Mercy," Nathan says. "I bet the part of our souls that remembers being them can be at peace if we find the whole story and work at changing the bad patterns and mistakes we made back then. I can't believe you're just going to give up now. Aren't you even willing to try?"

"You're too optimistic," I say. "You're too sure of a happily-ever-after ending." I stand to pace my room. I need to create some distance between us. I feel a tug toward Nathan that I need to ignore. Putting space between us will help me do that. "Nate did the same thing. He was so sure that all they had to do was run off together, and fate would take care of the rest. Mercy knew better. Mercy knew the world wasn't all optimism and rainbows. Storybook endings don't happen in real life, Nathan, and love rarely conquers all."

"I know I have to work on being more practical." He stands and leans against the post of my four-post bed. "That's one pattern I need to work on. I need to keep both feet on the ground. I lead with my heart more than my head."

"I'm the complete opposite." I keep my tone neutral. If I'm committing to Jay, I need to keep Nathan in the friend zone. "I lead with my head instead of my heart."

"Maybe we can both find a happy medium." Nathan sticks his hands in his pajama pants pockets and throws me a relaxed half-smile. "Maybe that's why fate brought us together again this time around. We're supposed to find balance together."

"We were brought together because you fell off the rotunda, and my dad gave you a good financial aid package." I know how harsh the words sound, but I'm hoping to jar some sense into him. "Not everything is about fate. Some things are just coincidence."

"I don't believe that." Nathan lifts his chin. "I don't believe in coincidence."

"Maybe you should believe and stop looking for patterns and symbols everywhere." I rub my eyes, exhausted by everything I'm expected to be. Dutiful daughter, girlfriend, straight A student, fixer of past-life patterns. Why can't anyone just let me be me for once and not stick a label on me?

He crosses the room in two long strides. "What's wrong with you tonight? Something's seriously off. What's going on?"

"Not everything is fated, Nate."

"There!" He points a finger at me. "You called me Nate again! I know we all have choices, Meredith, but can't you believe in this one little thing? Just this once, can't you believe just a little in fate and destiny? Is it really too much to ask?"

"Believe in the you-me together forever because we deserve a do-over because of the bum deal we got handed in the 1800s thing?" I rub my eyes again. If I could will myself into fainting, now would be an awesome time to do that to get out of this conversation. "No, Nathan, I don't think so. I can't. I'm sorry. It's too much to ask."

He ducks his head to see into my lowered eyes, but I turn my head away. "What is going on with you, Meredith? I thought we had something going here or, at the very least, a promise of something. When we kissed before, I felt the connection. It was more than just physical. Maybe I'm like Ritzi reading too much into things, so why don't you tell me what you think is going on. You seem able to turn your emotions on and off like a switch, but I'm not like that. Sorry if I'm too optimistic for you or try to see the good in people, but if you had the crap childhood I did, you'd want to look for the good. The alternative is not an option."

"Jay asked me to marry him." I spit out my news. I hold up my right hand with the enormous diamond ring weighing it down like an anchor. "It's more of a promise ring right now since I still have to finish school and he wants to make a name for himself in the pro tour, but I said yes. It's the right thing to do. There is no you and me, Nathan. There never was."

Nathan sucks in his breath. I can see the second the news registers because it's the second his face crumbles like the mountainside during a mudslide. "How can you be so cold?" he asks. "I thought I knew you better than that."

"You don't." My voice sounds emotionless and foreign even to my own ears. "No one does."

"So that's it, huh?" Nathan turns toward the door. I hold my breath to stop myself from calling out to him to stay. "That's it? You will take the easy way out and not even try to change the pattern?"

"It's what's right," I say. "I'm good at doing what's right."

"You're not doing what's right." Nathan turns to face me once more after opening the door and stepping into the hallway. "You're doing what's wrong but what everyone else thinks is right. You're not learning anything from the past, Meredith, because you're too afraid to disappoint the people in the present. Well, what about you? Why not try to make yourself happy for once instead of settling for disappointment? Try it. You might like it."

I sit on my bed after he's gone, his last words ringing in my ears. Am I really too afraid to disappoint people? At least if I'm the only one disappointed in myself, fewer people will get hurt. I wipe away tears. The only problem with that logic is I'm not the only one disappointed in myself tonight.

Nathan is disappointed in me too. And there's nothing I can do to fix it.

Chapter 28

It's one o'clock in the morning, and I'm still awake. I stare at the clock as if watching it switch from 1:00 to 1:01 will somehow make me sleepy. I replay my earlier conversation with Nathan in my head. Do I always take the easy way out just because I'm afraid to try the hard way? What's wrong with sticking with the familiar? It's got me through life just fine so far, so why should I change now? I bet Nathan would argue it's a pattern, and patterns can change, but why should I upend everything in my life just because he says so? Baby steps. I need baby steps.

It may not be the popular choice, but I like the straight and narrow, safe path. Nathan may call it the easy way out, but you don't have to think too hard or worry too much over decisions on the safe path. I don't like second-guessing myself and—until now—no one's ever questioned my choices. The second Nathan appeared, my life turned upside down. It's more than just the friction caused between Jay and me or, worse, among all three of us when we're together. Nathan is like the personification of my conscience. He tells me things about myself that I know but don't want to say out loud. He shines a light on all the things I don't like about myself like thinking with my head instead of my heart or deciding based on what will please Dad or Jay instead of what will make me happy. Is wanting to make others happy such a bad thing? So what if I forget myself. There could be worse things to push aside than your sense of self.

I need to sleep. Maybe the same relaxation techniques Catalina uses during the regression will work to help me sleep. What's the harm in trying? I close my eyes and take myself through the breathing techniques Catalina uses during the hypnosis sessions. It only feels like a few seconds before I fall asleep. But instead of the dreamless sleep I hoped for, I'm back in 1880s Haunting.

I'm standing by the retention wall of Stone Lake. There's a little boat half in, half out of the water with *Paradise Shores Hotel* painted on the side. The lake is choppy as usual, but the dark clouds signal a storm blowing in from the mountains. It makes the water churn and turn dark. It's not a good day for a boat trip. Everyone knows you're not supposed to go out on the lake when a storm is coming in from the mountains. The weather changes too fast. It can be sunny one second, and then lightning could strike the next. I want to call out to whoever plans to use the boat and tell them not to go out, but my voice doesn't work. I turn when I hear familiar voices. I would recognize them anywhere. I've heard them in my dreams and under regression enough by now. Nate and Mercy are standing close together near the boat, voices raised to a higher pitch as they continue to argue. For a second, I expect them to be in sepia tones like their pictures at Mrs. King's shop or an old-time movie, but here they are standing in front of me in living color. I hang back, unsure if they can see me or not.

"Did you think I wouldn't know?" Nate asks Mercy, his Irish accent thickening in his anger. "That I wouldn't find out? An engagement isn't somethin' you can hide away, Mercy. Especially from those gossip mongering chambermaids. Do you even know how much that silly little chit Abigail Purse enjoyed telling me the news?

They know how I feel about you. *Everyone* knows how I feel about you."

"Not everyone," Mercy says. "Papa and James are quite in the dark still."

"Everyone who matters knows." Nate pulls away when she reaches for his hand. "Below-stairs folks are worth a thousand Misters Stone and Piper."

Mercy steps away as if his words are a slap. "Thank you, Nate. You have just made my decision ridiculously simple. I planned to tell you James's token was just a promise ring—a promise I intended to break—but now, I believe I shall request the End of Season Ball be an Engagement Ball. Mine and James's Engagement Ball."

Nate sucks in his breath. "You don't mean that, Mercy. You don't."

"I do." She tilts her chin. I recognize the move because I did it less than a week ago. I also recognize the cold "watch me" tone since my voice has sounded the same way more often than I care to admit. "If you do not believe me, you are welcome to see with your own eyes at the end of the season. I believe you know the date? August 24."

"Your twenty-first birthday," he whispers.

"I would say I shall save you a place at our table, but I believe you will serve our table instead of sitting at it." Mercy is using her words now just for their power to hurt. How many times have I done the same thing with Jay and Nathan? Words are a powerful weapon. We feel their sting long after they die from our lips.

"How foolish I have been these last three years thinking there was hope." Nate's voice is as flinty as Mercy's. "You claim I have made your decision simple, Mercy, but you have made mine even simpler. Consider this my resignation. Goodbye, Miss Stone."

Despite the black, churning water and dark clouds gathering, Nate pushes the Paradise Shores boat into the water and climbs in. He raises the sail.

"Nate! Where are you going? Nate, it's too dangerous! If you're leaving, I'll get you a carriage. Nate!"

But the wind carries him away from the bay shore and Mercy's desperate calls. If he hears, he doesn't turn back like any sensible person would. As the boat and Nate get farther away and out of sight, Mercy falls onto the sand and cries.

"Nate! Nate!"

"Mercy?" I take a step closer. I don't know if I'm just seeing a memory or if I'm able to be a part of it and interact, but I'll test the boundaries of this dream and find out.

Mercy lowers her hands from her red, blotchy face. "Goodness! Who—what are you? Are you an angel?"

"No. I'm you, or, well, a future version of you. My name's Meredith."

She wipes under her damp eyes. "I am afraid I do not understand."

"Don't worry." I sit down next to her. "Sometimes I don't either. It's all really complicated for you and me."

Mercy examines my clothes. "If you are from the future, what are you doing here?"

"I'm trying to figure out the mistakes of my past, so I don't repeat them in the present." I hold my hands out palms up. "It's a lot harder than it sounds. Just when I think I have a handle on it, I fall into old patterns and get everyone mad at me. I feel like, no matter what, I keep making mistakes."

Mercy shakes her head again, blonde curls bouncing. "Pish. What a silly thing to say. We all make mistakes. That is how we learn."

"But I'm doomed to repeat my mistakes. Or your mistakes." I laugh. "I guess you could just call them *our* mistakes."

"You are an odd girl." Mercy turns her attention to the lake. "Nate will not really stay cross with me, will he? I did not mean it. I meant none of it."

"I'm sure he knows that." I pat her shoulder. I'm not used to comforting people, especially a version of me. "I know a boy a lot like your Nate in my time. His name is Nathan. Give Nate a day—maybe two, tops—and it will be like you never argued. Trust me on this one. He can't stay mad at you for long."

"I pray you are correct." She turns her head to study me like I'm something to be dissected in anatomy class. "What mistakes do you feel you are 'doomed to repeat?'"

I shrug. "I was hoping you could tell me."

Mercy thinks a moment. "If you know a boy like Nate, do not let him go as I did. Hold on tight because true happiness is rare to come by."

"What about James?"

She waves a hand. "James can find true happiness with a mirror. Everyone and everything is a possession to him—a symbol of status. Do you know someone like him as well?"

I nod. "The only difference is my James is named Jay. He's a good guy, though. He tries, at least. I think he's grown some since you knew him. You might like him."

Mercy chews her bottom lip. It's another habit I've picked up in the present. "Perhaps you mistake me. I do not dislike James, but the difference between Nate and James is like the difference between summer and winter. Is one season better than the other? No. Do I prefer one season over the other? Yes. There is no winner or loser, just a preference. I know that does not sound romantic, and I am sure the boys only see it in terms of black and white, but I..." She trails off. "Perhaps you understand?"

I nod. "More than you know. What should I do? What did you do?"

"My advice to you is to make sure you make wise choices," Mercy says. "I fear I have chosen poorly and shall live unhappily because of it. Do not let your Nate go as I did."

"You haven't lost him yet, Mercy."

She watches the water for any sign of the little sailboat. The water is as still and empty as a tomb. "I fear I have, Meredith. I fear I have."

Chapter 29

Something Nate said in the dream sticks in my mind. He said a nosey chambermaid named Abigail Purse told him about Mercy getting her engagement ring from James. Could it be *my* Abigail? I jump out of bed and grab my laptop. I boot it up and do a quick archives search of old newspapers until I find a copy of the paper we saw at Mrs. King's shop. I scan the grainy picture of the staff of the Paradise Shores Hotel. My eyes linger on Nate, so much like Nathan it's scary, before moving to examine the rows of chambermaids. I gasp. There. There in the second row, smiling like she doesn't have a care in the world, is Abigail. Did she really cause the final fight between Nate and Mercy? I don't want to believe it.

"Abigail!"

She appears at the summons. "Yes, miss?"

I spin my laptop around to show her the picture. "You were there. You were there the whole time and didn't tell me. You knew them. Nate even said you were some sort of spy that brought Mercy gossip to him and probably not in a good way. You did it for selfish reasons, didn't you?"

"No, miss, no." Abigail shook her head. "I loved Nate. Everything I did, I did out of love. For both of them. And now out of love for you and Nathan, miss. I want you to have the chance they didn't. I swear."

"Why didn't you tell me the truth?" I demand. "I trusted you just like Mercy did. If you loved Nate, does that mean you love Nathan too? Were you waiting around to stab me in the back just like you did Mercy?"

Abigail's mouth works for several moments before words come out. "Mercy was not the only one to love Nate, miss. He was nothing but loyal to her, though, so don't go thinking bad of him. Or Mr. Nathan for that matter. It was me reading too much into a kind word and gesture from Nate, nothing more. I know my chance at happiness with Nate is long past. No amount of wishing would ever make him mine. Not when Mercy was near. I accepted that, miss. If I couldn't be happy, I at least wanted Nate to have a chance to be. Who do you think helped sneak Mercy out through the servants' hall? Or delivered love letters late into the night? I did. I swear, miss, I put my own feelings aside and did everything I could to guarantee they stayed strong. It still didn't matter. I failed them, but, more than that, they failed each other."

"Why didn't you tell me any of this earlier?" I sink onto my bed. This story was getting more complicated by the second.

Abigail's form flickers. "It isn't my story to tell."

I replay her words in my mind. She loved Nate, but she tried to help him find happiness. And—*Reading too much into things.* Ritzi! Could Ritzi be Abigail reincarnated? The parallels are there. Liking a boy who likes someone else. Friends with the girl who is technically her competition. Trying to get the boy to notice her but still not succeeding. If I knew to look for the patterns, I'd have noticed them so much sooner.

"Abigail, do you think you've been reincarnated to do things over too?" I ask. "You know, to learn and grow like the rest of us?"

She wrings her hands in front of her. "I don't know, miss. I hope so."

I gesture at the door that leads to the bathroom that separates Ritzi's room from mine. "There's a girl next door named Ritzi. I think you'll find you have a lot in common with her."

Abigail looks at the door as if trying to decide if she should go haunt Ritzi for a bit or not. "Do you really think so, miss?"

I nod. "I know so. She won't be able to see or hear you, but you might find you have just as much of a chance of a do-over as the rest of us."

Abigail bobs a curtsy. "Oh, thank you, miss. I shall go visit her straight away." She floats across the room but stops and turns with one foot in the door. "Oh, and miss? I only did what I felt was right for Nate and Mercy. I thought it would push them together, not tear them apart. I hope, whatever you decide with your young men, you make the choice that is best for you and no one else."

"Thanks, Abigail." I smile as she fades through the door to explore her possible connection to Ritzi.

After she's gone, I grab my phone and call Nathan. It rings ten times before going to voicemail. Now it seems it's his turn to ignore me.

"Nathan, it's Meredith," I say to his voicemail. "Look, I'm really, really sorry if I pulled the Mercy-rich-girl-ice-princess routine on you last night. You're right about the pattern thing. I *am* repeating things, and I told myself I didn't care, but I do. I don't want to keep going in circles forever. I want to grow. I want to learn. I think we need to go back to Open Closed Doors to do that. We need to find out how Mercy and Nate's story ends. Even if there's not a you-and-me like how you want it to be, there is a you-and-me for setting the past free. I'll call Catalina to see when the next available appointments are. Call me when you get this, okay? I hope to talk to you soon. Bye."

I don't hold on to much hope of Nathan calling me back after how I treated him, but stranger things have happened. Even in Haunting.

Every text message alert and phone call send me scrambling for my phone, but none of them are from Nathan. Later in the afternoon, Jay shows up with a bag full of fast food and a promise of a picnic.

"Do we have to? I'm kind of waiting for someone to call me." I check my phone on the off chance that Nathan decided to text me in the two seconds between the time I checked my phone last and when Jay showed up.

"But I got food." Jay rattles the bag. "Do you seriously want to waste good food to sit on your phone all day?"

"Um, I don't know. Maybe?" I sneak a peek at my phone again.

Jay holds out his hand. He wiggles his fingers when I just stare at it. "Come on now. Give it here. Give me your phone." I hand it over. "You'll spend the afternoon with me and not think about your phone once, got it?"

As much as I'd like to hear from Nathan, it would be nice not to stress about it for a couple hours and just enjoy some time with Jay. Our relationship works best when we're alone. It's just when everything else gets in the way things fall apart. I reach back into my room and grab my purse. "Got it. I'm yours for the entire afternoon, phone-free."

"I hope you're mine for longer than that."

Jay wraps his arm around my waist as we walk, and I lean into him. I don't know where we're going, and I don't really care. I just like I can forget everything about school work, projects, and past lives, and relax—even if it's only for a couple hours. I'll take what I can get, even if it doesn't last.

We find a quiet spot on the quad under a tree. Jay unpacks the bag of food and hands me what he thinks I'll like. For someone who acts oblivious, he does a good job of remembering what I order when we go out. Maybe that's all the obliviousness is—an act.

"We should do this more often." Jay polishes off his burger in record time before moving on to his fries. "I like hanging with you, Mer. It makes me feel peaceful. Like nothing bad in the world can touch us."

I pick at my food. "Too bad we can't live in a bubble forever."

"What's stopping us?" Jay asks. "I mean, okay, sure, there's a lot of stuff stopping us, but those will not be factors forever." He touches the promise ring on my right-hand ring finger. "Do you mind moving this over to the left? I want to see what it looks like."

I do what I'm told without thinking and hold up my hand so that the sun glints off the diamond. How easy would it be just to say yes and forget about every other choice I'm expected to make? I could slide further into dutiful girlfriend-turned-fiancée mode and let Jay do all the deciding for me. It would be so easy. All it would take is one little word.

"Have you given any more thought to that?" Jay motions at the ring. "Making that permanent, I mean?"

"I didn't know promises came with an expiration date."

Jay realizes his mistake and backtracks. "It doesn't. It doesn't. I just wondered if you had thought about it, that's all. No rush. No pressure. Just wondering."

I move the ring back over to my right hand. "I'm happy to just keep it as a promise." I recognize how harsh that might sound to him, so I lean over and kiss the tip of his nose to soften my words. "When that changes, you'll be the first to know."

"I hope so." He wraps an arm around my shoulders, and I lean against his side. "We have a big meet next Saturday. I know you rarely like to come to my events, but it would be awesome if you could come watch this one. You're kind of my good luck charm. I always do better when you're there. Plus, we're almost engaged. It gives me the chance to show you and the ring off. What do you say? Will you come?"

If I let the promise ring turn into a full-fledged engagement ring, everyone will expect me to come to sporting events and whatever other career Jay pursues after retiring from skiing. I need to get used to the idea. "Um, sure."

Jay laughs. "You could at least try to sound enthusiastic, Mer."

"Saturday sounds great." I plaster on a big, cheesy grin for Jay's benefit. "It will be fun. I'll ride with the other ski groupies on the pep bus."

"The pep bus?" He grimaces. "Puh-leeze. If you don't mind getting to the course a little early, you can ride with me."

"If you're sure."

"If *I'm* sure?" Jay rolls his eyes. "Mer, I asked you to marry me. That's not something I take lightly. It's not like I'm running around campus tossing out rings to every girl I see." He cups the side of my face in one hand. "I want to spend my life with you. I'm pretty sure I can stand driving you to the ski meet."

"How can you be so sure of everything?" The words tumble out before I can check my filter and clamp down into dutiful-girlfriend mode again.

Confusion flows across Jay's face. "How can I be so sure of what?"

I pull back till we're not touching. I think better that way. When we're touching, it's too easy to remember the easygoing, mellow Jay who will do anything for me and allow myself to be the girl who just stays quiet and never speaks her mind. "How can you be sure that you want to spend your life with me? As far as I know, you've dated no one else. How can you know I'm the one—the epic beginning and end of your love-life universe—if you've never even looked at anyone else?"

"Where is all this coming from?" Jay asks. "I'm not blind. Of course I've looked at other girls. I've even talked to some Jay-you're-so-awesome-here's-my-number fangirls. I don't call or text them, though. I could have. But I didn't."

"Why not?" I ask.

"Because, when it comes down to it, they're not you. They're not *you*, Meredith. I don't know how many times or how many ways I have to tell you to convince you that I am committed to you. Is it really so hard to believe that I'd pick you over some groupies?"

I rub my sweaty palms down the front of my cargo pants. "Yes. No. I mean, I don't know. I just don't think I give you a whole lot to love most of the time."

Jay kisses me, feather light on the lips. "Well, you're wrong. The faster you get that thought out of your head, the better."

My text message alert goes off. Since Jay still has my phone, he checks it for me. I have my phone password protected so he can't read the message but can see who it's from.

"What's Vale doing texting you?"

"It probably has to do with our Colorado History project," I lie. "We're supposed to meet up this week to work out all the final details."

He hands over my phone. "You better answer that then."

I unlock my phone and check the text.

Nathan: *Stop. We need to just stop.*

I frown, forgetting Jay is even with me. I forget everything except that Nathan is hurting, and it's somehow all my fault.

Me: *Open appointment at Open Closed Doors, 4:00 Friday. Come with me.*

Nathan: *No.*

Me: *What do you mean, "no?"*

Nathan: *Goodbye, Meredith.*

Goodbye? What does he mean by goodbye? I look up, Jay coming into focus. "I should go." The lies continue to come far too easily. "Nathan has some questions about his section of the group project."

"Where are you meeting up?" Jay asks. "I'll walk you there."

"Uh, I shouldn't keep you from whatever you need to be doing." I say as I text *wait for me* to Nathan and hit send. "Don't worry about me. We can meet up later. Dinner maybe, or something else."

Jay grins. "I like the sound of 'something else.'"

I laugh. "I'll call you when I'm done with project stuff, okay?"

"Can't wait."

I leave Jay in the quad and head to the dorms, hoping he doesn't go back to his room before I have the chance to talk to Nathan. Sometimes it feels like I'm leading a double life, one I hope will soon converge so I don't have to keep all my stories straight. Maybe once Nathan and I find out what happened to Nate and Mercy and their spirits can rest, things can go back to normal—however one defines normal in this place. My life can't get much more complicated even if it tried.

"Nathan?" I knock on his dorm room door. "Let me in."

"Jay, how many times do I have to tell you to take your key?" Nathan calls from inside in answer to my knock. "I'm not always going to be here. I got a life too, you know." The door opens, and Nathan stares down at me. "Oh. You're not Jay."

"I came as soon as I could," I begin without preamble. "I'm worried about you, Nate." I close my eyes when I realize my slipup. "Nathan. I'm worried about you, Nathan. I must have called and texted like a million times. I thought you would be happy about me scheduling an appointment at Open Closed Doors. Why weren't you answering your phone?"

Nathan turns and heads back into the room. I follow. "I saw it was you and didn't pick up. Two can play the ice routine."

I run a hand through my hair. "That's not very nice, but since I was doing the exact same thing to you, I can't even pretend to be mad."

"So what made you change your mind about Open Closed Doors?" he asks.

"I want to find out what happened to Nate and Mercy," I say. "I don't want to keep repeating the cycle, Nathan. It hasn't worked out for anyone so far. We keep going around and around in circles. All it's brought is confusion. We need to put a stop to it now." I spy an open suitcase on his bed. "What's going on? Why are you packing?"

"'Cause I'm leaving." Nathan is not able to look me in the eye when he says it. "I don't belong here. Nate was an outsider and so am I. I'm so far down on the ski team alternate list, I'll never make it on the slopes, and you're parading around with a rock the size of Gibraltar on your hand. I don't fit into your world and never will. It's about time I stopped pretending and just leave you to your world and find my place somewhere else."

"But I don't want you to go." I reach for his hand. Nathan tries to pull away, but I hold on tight. "At least put your decision off through the weekend. Wait to see what we find out at our final regression appointment. Will you do that for me? Will you go one last time to Open Closed Doors?"

Nathan strokes my cheek with the fingers of his free hand. "Haven't you figured it out yet, Meredith? I'd do anything for you."

Despite all my brave talk of wanting to know what happened to Mercy and Nate, my feet once again stall outside the door of Open Closed Doors on Friday afternoon. It doesn't take a psychic or remembering Myrtle Stone King's words of "so many hearts broken" to know how things end.

"What's wrong?" Nathan turns his head to look at me, his hand hovering on the doorknob. "Is it more of the same like last time? I'm here, remember? I'm always here for you."

"I'm scared." Just saying the words out loud makes the fear lose a little of its power. "I know any life is not all sunshine and light, but, sometimes, it feels like it's easier not to know. Maybe we forgot for a reason. Have you ever thought of that? Maybe we're pushing where we shouldn't push." I glance at the quiet graveyard next to the shop. It looks peaceful, but the voices of the dead are still reaching out to me, asking for help. They're just a whisper. If I let my guard down, they'll become deafening. I can't help everyone. Maybe I can try to help myself. I turn back to Open Closed Doors. Is exploring the past the only way to do that? Is this the only way to set Mercy and Nate free?

"Maybe the 'what happened' is the puzzle piece we've both been searching for." Nathan opens the door. He's sure, even if I'm not. "After that, everything else will fall into place. We'll be able to see the big picture and decide what to do after that."

"I hope you're right." I force my legs to move and follow him inside.

"Welcome back." Catalina smiles when the bell jingles our entrance. She punches the button on the phone system to send calls to voicemail and sets out the sign that reads, *In a session—please relax and be patient.* "I hope you've been able to apply some of the knowledge you've uncovered so far."

"It's easier to pick up on the patterns," Nathan says. "If we're doing the right thing with that knowledge is a different story."

Catalina leads us into the back room. I look at the familiar recliner as if it's somehow my enemy now instead of the way to get the answers I seek. I thought I was ready to do this, but now I'm not so sure. If you face the fact that someone is dead, it means they're truly gone.

"It's okay. You can do this. Just relax." Nathan squeezes my shoulder when he notices my hesitation.

"One of the good things about hypnosis is it's a relaxation technique," Catalina adds to help calm my jitters. "If you just listen to my voice and focus on your breathing, all your fears and worries will disappear while you're under."

"Can you put a little something on the end of the bringing-me-out-of-it script to help me feel surer or at peace or make better choices or something?" I ask. "I don't think I'm doing the best I can with any of those."

"I can suggest it, but it's up to you to follow it," she says. "The choices you make, even if they seem wrong, are the best for you. Life itself is a learning experience. Every choice we make, from what color shirt we wear to who we pick as our parents before birth, all influence what we learn in life. Some have bigger consequences than others, but we live so we can learn."

I take the blanket Catalina offers once I sit in the recliner and pull it up over my legs and skirt. If it had been my choice, I would have worn pants to school. But I've never questioned Dad's interference on everything in my life from what I wear to which boy I date. Maybe I should. Maybe I should question everything in my life. If I question my choices, would I learn more?

"Why am I so afraid?" I ask.

"Facing the truth of our actions and the resulting consequences is never easy." Catalina pops a cassette tape into the recorder and hovers her pen over the pad of paper. "You're doing the right thing, Meredith, by coming here and exploring your past life. By understanding why you're stuck in these soul-patterns, you can let go, heal the pain of the past, and move on. Are you ready?"

I don't feel ready, but I nod anyway. "Whenever you are."

I listen to Catalina's practiced, soothing voice and focus on my breathing. I breathe in relaxation and breathe out tension. I feel the calming warmth spread through my body as it makes each section from head to toe heavy during the deepening, and, finally, I'm in the private elevator going down, down, down to the circular library of memories. I've stayed away from the "bad memory" books until now. I hesitate for just a moment before I reach for the nearest one. It's time. I need to know what I've felt so afraid to face.

Haunting
August 24, 1888
Mercy Stone

"Today is my birthday." I watch my reflection in the mirror as my maid Abigail fastens the sapphires I am to wear tonight at the End of Season Ball about my neck.

"Happy birthday, miss." She bobs a low curtsy. "The sapphires are an excellent choice. They match your eyes. I dare say Mr. Piper won't be able to take his eyes from you tonight."

"That is the goal." I wish to say more, but I am unsure how to broach the subject. Abigail and I rarely gossip. She is quite the help when I need to skulk about the hotel undetected, yet I cannot just up and ask leading questions without appearing suspicious or—worse— jealous. "Abigail?" I ask. "You are friendly with the other maids, are you not?"

"Some, miss," she replies. "Others? Well, others are too much the gossipmongers for even me to find pleasant. They jump on any little shred of scandal and tear it apart."

"Like Madeline Pruitt." I remember Nate's contempt for the snubbed-nosed little chambermaid who would rather have him all to herself rather than let me turn his head.

"Rightly so, miss. If I may say so, she is quite a horrid little thing."

"So they have told me." I finger the sapphires around my neck, finding comfort in their cool smoothness. "Have the other servants spoken at all of Nate? Has anyone had any word from him? It seems strange and so very unlike him to shirk his duties to the hotel and to, well, me. You are my eyes below stairs, Abigail. Please, if you know anything—anything at all—tell me."

"No one has heard anything about Nate, miss." Abigail checks and double-checks that my hair is styled to perfection. "I wish I had some news to give you. Perhaps he went back to the rails. I've heard that's what the rest of the kitchen staff speculate."

"But it is so unlike him to not send word to anyone. He should know I—*they*—would worry."

"Perhaps he has just been overwhelmed and unable to send a cable."

"I hope so," I sigh. "I dearly hope so."

"Mercy, dear." Papa knocks on my door. "It is time."

I turn to Abigail and engulf her in a swift embrace. "You have always been so loyal. Thank you."

"You're welcome, miss."

"If you hear word of Nate—anything at all—please tell me," I request. "Interrupt a dance if you must, but I need to know."

"Of course, miss."

I smooth my hands down my skirt to make sure everything is in order before moving across the room to open my door. I smile at Papa as if there is nothing on my mind save an evening of dancing and flirting with James Piper. How can I really tell him I am heartsick over the fact it has been three days without word from Nate? Three days! Three days ago, he pushed that boat out onto the lake, and we have not heard word since. My mind is in such a whirl that even my dreams are muddled. I dreamed of a strange girl with peculiar clothes. I woke the next morning with more questions than answers.

"Happy birthday, darling." Papa kisses my cheek before tucking my arm close. He leads the way to the staircase and grand ballroom below and stops right before we enter. I can see the dancers and musicians below, enjoying the night without a care in the world. I search for Nate in the crowd of kitchen staff weaving through the party guests, offering champagne and hors d'oeuvres, but I might as well be searching for a ghost. He is not here. I press my fist against my aching heart.

"Is there anything the matter, darling?" Papa asks.

"No, Papa," I answer. "I am overwhelmed, that is all. It is a beautiful ball. You have truly outdone yourself."

He sweeps an arm to show off the crowd below. "It is all for you, my dear. All for you."

Now, more than ever, I wish it was not for me. I wish I lived a simple life with a simple boy and did not have to be tied to society's rules. But it feels as if someone tied a rock around my neck that weighs me down. I cannot escape it, no matter how hard I try.

Papa propels me toward the grand staircase to make our even grander entrance. As if on cue, the musicians stop playing when Papa and I appear on the top step. The gathered guests turn and clap as we descend to the tune of "Happy Birthday." It seems silly to make such a fuss over something as simple as turning twenty-one, but I know it means I am of age and prime for marriage. If James was not such an attractive candidate for my hand, I feel Papa would try to auction me off to the highest bidder. I stumble, feeling faint, as we finish our descent. James steps from the crowd and bows. If he notices my unsteady appearance, he does not comment on it.

"May I have the honor of the first dance, Miss Stone?"

He kisses my gloved hand when I hold it out to him. "You may, Mr. Piper."

James leads me out onto the floor for a waltz. The assembled guests take this as their cue to find partners. As we settle into the steps and music, I relax. James really is a glorious dancer. No matter why Papa wishes me to spend time in his company, I cannot fault him for his skill on the dance floor. I am in good hands and company as we float across the ballroom. Even so, it feels all wrong. James is not the one I want to dance openly with. Nate is.

"I have been thinking of the perfect time to make our announcement," James says as we twirl about the floor. "People expect an early announcement, but I say let's leave them hanging until the end. It will build the suspense and make them think you have jilted me instead of agreeing to be mine."

"It will be the talk of the society pages once the guests return east," I agree.

"Exactly." James smiles as if it is all a silly game to him instead of our lives and future at stake. "I'm glad you have agreed to our union," he adds. "Uniting the families will be beneficial for all involved."

"I hope love comes into play somewhat, James," I remind him. "We should build any sort of attachment on love and not just money."

"Love?" His fair brow furrows like it is a foreign concept. "Naturally, love is very important to a union, but it is not the only deciding factor when choosing a life mate. The quality of the person and their family is paramount, I believe. I thought we agreed on this, Mercy."

"You make it sound like a business deal," I accuse.

"It is," he says. "Marriage is like merging two companies. There must be something beneficial in the deal for each, or it will fall through. I know divorce is all the rage in some eastern circles, but I shan't have the taint of scandal touch my family's name. When we marry, it will be forever. There will be no going back."

"So, even if we found we chose unwisely and realized it was a mistake, there would be no outlet?" I am not altogether sure I like this new aspect of James emerging.

"There are other outlets acceptable to an empty marriage besides divorce," he answers.

I shudder at his words. "You speak of dalliances. What of the wedding vows? It is a sin to break them."

"Depending on the situation. Even St. Peter himself would turn a blind eye to certain 'dalliances' as you call them."

I pull my hands free as the music stops. "Forgive me, James. I am feeling ill. I need some air."

I push my way through the crowd to the little door leading to the veranda. Once outside, I take big gulps of the cool night air. Must I truly saddle myself to James Piper for eternity? Oh, where is Nate when I truly need him?

I hear a commotion from the kitchen and move to investigate since the veranda extends the length of the grand ballroom and to the adjoining kitchen.

". . . I scarce believed it meself until I saw the proof. All puffed up like one of them blowfish from too long in the drink. He had sense enough to store identification in his inside pocket, or the coppers woulda had a time identifying him."

"Identifying whom?" I feel as if I am walking through a dream as I enter the kitchen from the veranda entrance. "What are you all gossiping about when you should work?"

"Oh, Miss Stone!" Cook's hand flies to cover her mouth. "You needn't be in here. Off with you now. Enjoy your party." She makes a shooing motion with her apron. "Off you go. Let us take care of the details in here."

I shake my head. "Not until you tell me whom you are speaking of. Please, Cook," I add when she looks reluctant. "You have known me since I was a child. I used to eat bread and butter in this very kitchen and help you bake pies. Please. Tell me."

"Very well." She sighs, not relishing the task at hand. "They've found Nate Thatcher. Drowned, God rest his soul."

"Drowned?" My knees give way, and I grab onto the counter for support. "Are you positive? Are you positive it was Nate Thatcher?"

"Bless me, child, I saw him with my own eyes." Cook makes the sign of the cross over her head and chest. "I wouldn't believe it otherwise."

"Drowned," I repeat as if saying it once more will make it seem real. "Drowned. Forgive me, Cook, I must go."

I lurch out of the kitchen. I'm not sure where I expect my feet to take me but do not care as long as it is far away from the news of Nate's fate.

"Mercy? Mercy, wherever were you?" Papa asks as I careen into the grand ballroom. "Mercy?"

I attempt to push past him but stumble. Papa grabs ahold of my arm. "I must get upstairs before I am unable." I press at my chest, knowing my eyes must appear desperate when they meet Papa's concerned face. "Please, Papa, I must get upstairs. Please, don't stop me. Please. I must get upstairs."

"There she is! Darling, come and share the happy news! I can't wait another second!" James signals the band to play a sentimental song as he takes my hands and pulls me out onto the middle of the dance floor amidst both mine and Papa's protests.

"Please, James, no, I cannot." I shake my head, one fist over my heart. James ignores my protests. Instead, he turns to the gathered crowd and raises a glass of champagne.

"Honored guests, friends, and family, I am overjoyed to announce that Mercy has agreed to make me the happiest man alive. May I present my future wife, the love of my life, Miss Mercy St—"

I collapse on the dance floor. I stare up at the painted ceiling with its cherubs and angels, praying they take me away as they did Nate. I hear James's voice as if it is coming from far away.

"Mercy? Mercy? Give her air! Give her air, I say!"

Air? How can I breathe without Nate? How can I even live without my Nate?

"Mercy? Mercy, can you hear me? Mercy? Mercy!" James's voice fades even more into the background.

I see Nate just beyond reach, moving among the guests.

"Nate?" I smile. "Nate, do not leave me. Come back. Please, do not leave me."

I close my eyes, and he is suddenly beside me. There is a soft glow about him, like in a religious painting, but his smile is the same as always as he holds out a hand to me. "I'm here, Mercy. I'm here."

I take his hand, feeling light as air. Everything else—the party, Papa, James—seems a long way off. They don't matter anymore. The only thing that matters is Nate, and he will never let go of my hand again.

"Are you sure you're okay?" Nathan asks for what must be the fiftieth time since we left Open Closed Doors. He's driving Dad's car since I don't feel up to it after experiencing Mercy finding out about Nate's death, and then seeing her own death in the regression. "'Cause you're quiet. If you're not okay, just say so. I'm not sure what I can do, but we can figure something out, okay? Just say the word and we'll figure something out, okay?"

"She died. She died on her birthday. She died on her birthday." I'm fixated on that fact almost as much as Nathan is fixating on asking me if I'm okay.

"I know. That was pretty intense," he agrees. "Do you think it was the shock of finding out about Nate that caused something to happen, or was there some sort of underlying condition no one knew about?"

I close my eyes and think back to what I saw under regression. Mercy was putting her hand over her heart and, at least in her mind, complaining about her heart hurting. Could it be more than just being heartsick over not knowing where Nate was? "I wish I knew.

She died on her birthday. Her twenty-first birthday. What if I die on my twenty-first birthday?"

"You won't die on your twenty-first birthday." Nate tries to take me out of being fatalistic.

"How do you know?" I wave my hands like I have a cramp in them and need to get circulation back, or as if by feeling them move, it can help convince me I'm real—that *this* is all real—and I'm not that girl dying on a ballroom floor anymore. "How do you know I'm not just going to drop dead in a couple years? Mercy didn't start her day off thinking, 'Hey, this seems like a good day to die.' She woke up and got ready for a party. She got engaged to James. She found out about Nate drowning. We don't plan for death. We don't plan for any of this. How do you know I won't die on my birthday like Mercy did? How do you know I won't die tomorrow?"

Nathan pulls down a side street and stops the car. "I don't, okay? I don't have the answers to any of those questions. No one does. Do you remember what Catalina said? All our choices, all our lives, are learning experiences. I think it was meant to happen. I think Nate was meant to take the boat out that day and drown just like Mercy was supposed to die on her birthday. As crappy an ending as it was for both, I think it still needed to happen so we can learn from it now. Life is one big learning experience. Some lessons are harsher than others and take longer to work out, but we still learn from them. That's all we can do. Learn."

"What can we learn from two people not that much older than us dying sudden, tragic deaths?"

"It's not what we can learn from their deaths but from their mistakes." Nathan twists to face me. "In your dream, Mercy told you not to let 'your Nate' go. She meant me. That's what everything we keep running up against and all these signs and insights seem to be pointing at. We can't let each other go. That's what Nate and Mercy did and look what happened to them. We need to learn from the past, not repeat it."

"But we barely know each other." My head gets in the way of my heart as usual. I'm used to being the practical, do-as-I'm-told, not what-I-feel, good girl, and that will not change just because I've been running around some metaphysical shops with the new kid at school.

"We do know each other." Nathan grabs my hand. "I've told you before, Meredith, I'd know you anywhere. You feel it too. I know you do."

I don't pull my hand away like I should, but my tone is not encouraging either. "We don't know each other, Nathan. Not really. I won't listen to any of this my-soul-called-to-yours-across-the-ages nonsense either. Do you know how much that sounds like a cheesy pickup line? We—Meredith Monroe and Nathan Vale—barely know each other. I've been dating Jay for two years and agreed to wear his promise ring. He'd like me to promise to make it more but I don't know. I need to think about it. No matter what I decide, I don't want to jump out of one relationship and into another. Both of you might need to give me some space to think."

Nathan keeps his voice calm and even. "I'm not using Mercy and Nate as an excuse or a cheesy pickup line. I just think we should take in what we've learned so we can break the patterns. I don't want you to pick Jay because you feel like it's your duty or responsibility or like you somehow owe it to him. That's reasonable, right? Even if you choose not to make a choice at all, that's up to you."

"I don't know what I want to do about Jay, but I don't think I'm ready to break up with him just yet. I might be later, or he might break up with me, but I just don't know yet. I need more time. From both of you."

"If you want to be friends for now, I can deal." Despite his words, I see a flash of disappointment streak across his face. At least he's trying to be noble about things and not dish out ultimatums as some guys might do. "Being your friend is better than not being in your life at all, so I can deal. If Jay is who you think you want, I'll respect that. I'll give you space, I'll give you time, I'll give you anything you want, Meredith, just promise me you'll decide what's right for you instead of what's right for everyone else this time around. Learn from Mercy. Promise me that, okay?"

What's right for me? After so long of doing what's right for everyone else and never thinking of myself, I'm not really sure, but I can try. I can definitely try.

"Promise me," Nathan repeats when I take too long to answer.

I nod. "I promise."

"Hey, there's my favorite girl." Jay smiles as I slip into the passenger seat of his Camaro Saturday morning to ride to the ski meet with him. It still floors me how something as simple as seeing me makes him light up with happiness. Maybe if I had a higher opinion of myself, I'd see it. "I know skiing isn't that exciting to you, Mer, but I can't tell you how much this means to me to have you cheering me on."

"I'm happy if you're happy." The words sound trite, but I say them anyway. If I ever learn to stand up for myself, I'll need to stop saying what I think people want to hear all the time and just be honest with them—and with myself.

"I hear some pros will be there watching us." Jay chatters away as if I said nothing. "You know, sizing up the hot, young talent, checking out their competition, all that good stuff. I can't wait to win big and show them what's coming up on the circuit next season. Hey, change of plans. I know I said I'd announce I'm going pro after graduation, but I thought it would be more dramatic and, you know, more media will cover it, if I announce after I win the meet. What do you think?"

"What if you don't win?" I ask.

Jay looks at me like I just asked about the possibility of Colorado not getting snow in the winter. "What do you mean what if I don't win? I always win—especially if you're watching. You're my good luck charm." I open my mouth to protest, but he waves away my words. "I know, I know. You don't get up to the slopes to watch me compete much, but just knowing you're thinking of me and there for me in spirit really makes a difference. It keeps me focused, you know? I want to be someone that you can be proud of. I want to give you a good life. That's why, after I win, I plan to raise my trophy, grab the mike, and announce to everyone I'm going pro after graduation. You'll be by my side, won't you? Athletes with blonde girlfriends or wives do better in their sport. It's totally a real statistic. I saw it on Sports Center."

"Jay, those athletes do better because they *are* better, not because their wife or girlfriend is blonde," I say.

"Well, they're supportive, and that's the big thing that matters to me," he says. "You'll support me, right, Mer? Even if I'm traveling the world and can't see you all the time like we're used to?"

I pull my legs up to my chest and wrap my arms around them. "Graduation is months off, Jay. Do we need to talk about this now?"

"We need to talk about it sometime." Jay pulls into the parking lot of the ski slope where the meet is held but doesn't get out of the car. "Graduation may seem like a long way off to you, but it's under six months for me. That will go by fast, Mer. Faster than we think."

I distract myself from giving him an answer by looking around. The location is just a big hill, some bleachers for fans, and white tents for trophies and refreshments. I'm not a fan of the cold, so hanging out watching people ski has never been my idea of a fun time. "We'll talk about it," I say. "Just not right now."

"If not now, when?"

"After the meet. I promise."

We climb out of the car. Jay grabs his ski gear from the back seat. I pull my wool newsboy cap as far down on my head as it will go and wrap my scarf around my neck a couple extra times for warmth. I can't get excited about being here. I should cheer until my voice is hoarse with the rest of the ski groupies. I should have a huge sign with some cute slogan on it or a giant picture of Jay that I spent hours making by hand. I should have been up all night puff-painting a "Jay's #1" t-shirt that I'd display despite the freezing temps and little news coverage. Instead, I barely manage a smile when a local reporter asks Jay and me to pose for a picture and give a quote for his write-up on the event. After telling the reporter that I support Jay "no matter what" and "of course I think he will win because he's amazing at whatever he does," Jay leaves me at the stands with a kiss and the promise to find me after the results are final. I buy a cup of hot chocolate and settle in to watch the meet.

I know little about skiing, but I do know there's a reason Jay could have skipped his final year of school and turned pro this year instead of waiting. He's amazing. A prodigy. Once he's down the slope, everyone else might as well pack up and go home. He cruises through the competition, beating his nearest opponent by eight seconds.

Jay finds me in the tent buying another hot chocolate. "Hey, babe, were you watching the whole time? It was one of my best runs ever." He kisses me, still pumped from his win. "I really showed those pros in the audience who to watch out for on the tour next season. Look out, world. Jay Jameson is on the scene."

"You were great." I turn my head so that he only gets my cheek when he leans in for another kiss. "Um, Jay, can we, um, can we have that talk now? The one you wanted in the car but I wanted to wait on?"

He looks around to make sure we're the only ones in the white tent. When another group comes in to get refreshments, he takes my hand and leads me out of earshot, which I'm grateful for I don't plan to be yelling, but I don't want anyone to overhear us, either.

"Okay, what gives?" Jay asks once we're a safe distance away from anyone that might hear us. "Does this have anything to do with Vale?"

Jealousy does not look good on Jay. I pull my arm free but don't answer the question. Why does he always bring up Nathan? Can't he see that we had problems long before Nathan showed up?

"Well, does it?" Jay demands.

"No!" I shout. "Why would you bring up Nathan at a time like this? This has everything to do with you and me, Jay, and nothing with him. Leave Nathan out of it."

Jay grabs my arm again and leads me further away from the tent and the now-curious gawkers. So much for not raising our voices or causing a scene. "Why wouldn't I bring him up? I have eyes, Meredith. I knew from the second Vale came into our lives that he's been after you. He hasn't made it a secret. What have you done to discourage him? Nothing. How do you think that makes me feel?" He gestures toward the dwindling crowd in the stands. "I have a line of girls a mile long just begging for my attention, and the one girl I want—the one girl I need—acts like I'm invisible. Guess what? I have Nathan friggin' Vale to thank for that. There're three people in this relationship, not two."

"Stop dragging Nathan into our problems," I hiss. "This has nothing to do with him. I told you before, it is you and me, Jay, so leave him out of it."

"See!" he cries. "You're *still* defending him! I can't believe he sent you out to fight his battles. Where is he?" Jay looks around like he expects Nathan to jump out from behind a tree. "Is he waiting in the parking lot so you can ride off into the sunset together, laughing over poor Jay's busted-up heart?" He grabs my arms above the elbows, squeezing a little too hard.

"Jay! Jay, you're hurting me."

His eyes go wide as if he just realized what he did. His fingers open, and we both step back in opposite directions. "I-I-I'm sorry, Mer. I didn't mean it. I don't know why I did that. I swore to myself I'd never act like him. I'd never act like my dad and then...and then I *do*. You're never going to forgive me, are you? I wouldn't forgive me if I were you. You don't need my frickin' baggage. I don't even want it."

"Jay, you are not your father." I reach a hand out and lay it across his cheek, hoping my touch might make the words sink in faster. "And I'm not breaking up with you."

His brow and lips pucker in confusion. "You're not?"

"No, I'm not. I just need to change our dynamics a little." I take off his promise ring and hold it out to him. "I should give this back to you, though. I don't want to break up, but it's a good idea if we slow things down." I look at the ring he hasn't made a move to take back. So many promises wrapped up in a piece of jewelry that I don't know I'll be able to keep. "Everything got really confusing really quick once I started exploring my connection to Mercy. I don't know what's going on, but it's not fair to any of us if I just ignore what I learned or Nathan's part in it. Just like it's not fair to any of us if I ignore what I feel for you either, Jay. I know that's not quite the answer you want to hear. It's complicated and doesn't involve you and me running off to some mountain cottage together, but it's the truth. I want to be honest with you. I should have been honest with you from the start. I'm sorry if I haven't been. I do want to be with you, but all this future-promise-marriage talk is scaring me. It's making me shut down instead of going all in like you deserve. I don't want to do that to you. Until I know for sure I can go all in, I need to take a step back and take things more casual rather than committed." I bite down hard on my bottom lip. "You've been nothing but patient with me, Jay, with not a whole lot in return, but this is what I want."

Jay curls my fingers around the ring before leaning forward to kiss my forehead. "It's a lot better than where I thought the conversation was going."

I breathe a sigh of relief. "You mean it?"

Jay pockets the ring. He closes his eyes and takes deep breaths in and out. When he opens his eyes, I can tell he puts on a brave face for me. Not for himself—for me. Jay motions at my arms. "I'm sorry I grabbed you like that, Mer. I'm not like my dad. I promise."

"I know you're not," I assure him. "Are you really cool with taking a step back and being more casual instead of committed? You can tell me the truth, Jay."

He closes his eyes again, thinking. When he opens them, he nods. "Not really, but I think I can be. And, Mer, about the whole shutting-down thing? I get it. You may think I don't, but I do. You're scared and confused, and that's why you shut down. I should have been there for you. I should have recognized it, and I didn't. I was so caught up in my own petty feud with Vale that I forgot about what you were going through. I'm sorry, Mer. I won't let it happen again. If you want to slow things down, we slow things down." He taps the pocket holding the promise ring. "Remember this is waiting for you, just like I am."

I blink back tears before throwing my arms around his neck. "Oh, Jay! I don't deserve you!"

"Sure you do," he whispers close to my ear, though I feel he's talking to himself instead of me. "You just won't let yourself believe it yet."

As we're clinging to each other, a voice comes over the loudspeaker announcing, "Now it's time to award our trophies!" I pull back before Jay does, feeling embarrassed that now of all times is when the emotional floodgates break down.

"They'll call your name soon." I watch as the sixth and fifth place finishers accept the awards. "Do you want me to wait in the parking lot?"

"Will you stand up there with me?" he asks. "I appreciate your support, Meredith, no matter how you choose to give it."

I take his offered hand, and we walk up on stage side by side as they announce Jay as the winner. He coaches me to just relax and smile as camera flashes go off from the media and fans. Can I get used to a life of this? Jay oozes charisma while I feel as invisible as the ghosts in the Haunting cemetery. As much as he talks about wanting a simple life somewhere with just the two of us, would he give up all this fame and fortune for me?

Chapter 35

Jay drops me off at campus before heading to the ski team victory party. For the first time, I don't feel awkward or on edge on what's expected of me with saying goodbye. Do I kiss him? Do I not kiss him? It doesn't matter. I make up my own rules now. It's my life. I'll live it how I want from now on.

Abigail is waiting for me in my dorm room. I jump back before realizing it's just her. Some ghosts are not as friendly around town. I motion for her to come away from the open bathroom suite door. If Ritzi is home, she might overhear what, to her, looks like me talking to myself.

"What are you doing here?" I whisper. "I thought you were hanging with Ritzi now."

"I can see glimpses of myself in her, miss, but she can't hear me," Abigail says. "How am I supposed to guide her from my mistakes if we can't communicate? Even if she could hear me, how do I make her understand I don't want my regrets to become her regrets?"

"I'll buy Ritzi a Ouija board." I'm only half-joking.

Abigail shakes her head. "No, miss. Those are not toys. Certain darknesses might slip through no matter how pure your intentions."

"What about a séance?" I like the idea the second it comes to me. "Ritzi is planning to demonstrate a Victorian séance for our living history project. You just need to make sure you're the spirit that comes through and... there you go. Communication."

"Perhaps." She doesn't sound convinced. She lowers her gaze, catching sight of my jewelry-free hand. "Oh, miss, are you choosing Mr. Nathan? Mercy would be so pleased."

"I'm choosing neither." I hate to spoil her excitement. "I'm choosing not to decide yet. In a way, I guess, I'm choosing me. I want to do what makes me happy instead of what makes everyone else happy. That's not a bad thing, is it?"

"No, miss," Abigail agrees. "I think Mercy would be right proud of your decision."

"Abigail?" I'm not sure how to ask my next question but decide to try my best anyway. "Why is it that the ghosts I want to see the most—my mom, Mercy, Nate—never come around?"

"They must be at peace, miss," she says. "I believe you've helped Mercy and Nate in that regard. It's only us restless spirits that stick around longer than we have to."

"What can I do to help you be at peace, Abigail?"

"Nothing, miss." She nods toward Ritzi's room. "By helping her, I believe I'll help myself find peace."

I smile. I'd hug Abigail, but I know my arms will go right through her. "Thank you for being my friend. I better talk to Nathan now. He needs to know my decision too."

"Good luck, miss."

I turn when I'm at the door, my hand hovering above the doorknob. "Thanks, Abigail. Good luck with Ritzi. I hope you find your peace."

She bobs a curtsy before disappearing.

Nathan opens the dorm room when I knock. "Where's Jay?"

"Out getting pizza with the rest of the main team and the adoring masses after another crushing victory," I say. "He dropped me off at campus. Can I come in?"

He steps aside and makes a sweeping gesture with his arm. I glance at his empty, still-made bed.

"No suitcase. Are you staying?"

Nathan points at my right-hand ring finger. "No ring? Did you break up with Jay?"

I run a hand through my hair. It feels naked without Jay's ring on it. "I feel like we should play rock, paper, scissors to decide who talks first. I have questions, you have questions. Who goes first?"

"Ladies first."

I smack his arm. "You just want to know what happened with Jay!"

Nathan flashes an embarrassed grin before sitting on his bed. "Well, I'd be lying if I said I wasn't curious, but if you want me to go first, I'll go first. One thing I've learned from Nate is not to run from my problems, so I'm not running. I'm sticking it out here and will fight. For you, for me, and for everything I want and think I deserve in this life. Besides, I can't leave you and Ritzi in the lurch for our group project. She says she has something killer for the séance part of the presentation."

My heart beats a little faster with just a twinge of jealousy at the mention of Ritzi's name. "Have you, uh, talked to her? She was a little confused with where things stood with you and her."

Nathan shrugs. "She might still be confused. I don't know about Ritzi, but I'm keeping things in the friend zone. What did you decide?" he asks. "About Jay, I mean."

I sit next to him on the bed. "One thing I learned from Mercy is not to follow my head so much instead of my heart, so I followed my heart." I twist my hands in front of me. "It feels a little weird to make decisions based on what makes me happy instead of what makes everyone else happy, but I think I can get used to it. Jay and I didn't break up. Not completely, at least. I asked to slow things down to casual, and he agreed. I feel a little selfish coming here and going, 'Hey, I didn't completely break up with my boyfriend, but maybe I can date both of you to figure out if one of you has an advantage.' Casual sounds worse when I say it out loud. I don't mean I will be running around dating half the ski team. I just mean I want you both to know there's an even playing field. I want it out in the open, so no one feels like they have to sneak around and lie to anyone. Is that selfish?" I chew on my bottom lip. "Am I selfish?"

"It's not selfish to grab onto happiness when it's right in front of you." Nathan lifts his hand like he wants to touch my cheek or hair before thinking better of it and letting the hand drop to his side. "I can be patient, Meredith. I can give you all the time you feel you need to straighten everything out in your heart and head. If you want casual, I can do casual. For me, it'll be a relief to be more out in the open like that. I won't have to hide or feel guilty that I feel this way in the first place because you're someone else's girlfriend. I know Jay doesn't believe in the metaphysical or past lives, but he's a part of this just as much as we are. We can figure it out together this time. All three of us." Nathan grins. "And will you please promise to get that damn cup of coffee with me already? I've been asking forever."

I laugh. "Fine. But only one cup."

"I'll take what I can get."

We somehow laugh until we fall back together on the bed. Nathan kisses me, and I melt into him, feeling as if I've been denying myself something my soul has been craving for far too long. I know we've kissed before, but that felt secret and hidden and guilt-ridden. Now I've taken a step back from my relationship status with Jay, I don't have that burden of guilt when I'm with Nathan. I feel free. I could *definitely* get used to this.

I bury my face in his chest. He smells like laundry detergent and dry erase markers. I smile to myself, embarrassed that ice princess Meredith definitely seems to have taken a permanent vacation with both Jay and Nathan. Did breaking out of my box by making choices for me and me alone really create such changes in a short amount of time? I should have done this *years* ago.

But you didn't know Nathan years ago, a voice in my head whispers. That's true. Maybe now is the right time. Maybe I wasn't ready before, and now I am. There's no time like the present—that's a lesson I learned from the past. Seize the day and all that.

"What are you thinking about?" Nathan whispers.

"You mean when I can string a coherent thought together?" I prop myself up on my elbows. "I was thinking about all the things I've learned about myself in a short amount of time. All the soul-patterns we've recognized and corrected. I didn't know I was going around in a circle until the truth was laid out in front of me. I know I've made more mistakes than I care to admit, Nathan, but I promise not to make the same mistake twice." I swipe my finger across my heart in an X gesture. "Cross my heart."

Nathan presses a kiss onto the center of my forehead when I lean into him again. "We all learn from our mistakes. It just took us one hundred and twenty years to learn from ours."

I sigh and cuddle closer to Nathan. The Night That Changed Everything—that changed my life four years ago—also brought me so much more. I can see that now. I used to think being a medium made me a freak. Now, I see it gives me the ability to help people. Those people may not be alive, but they need help all the same.

There is also that nagging thought that I haven't brought up with Nathan since the day at the hospital—who or what pushed him over the railing? Who wanted to be sure we met and changed the future? Am I brave enough to find out?

But I can't be afraid anymore—not of whoever stalked us to make sure we met, or of the graveyard. This gift that I used to think of as a curse can bring them peace and closure. Why should I hide from that? The ghosts around this town need me. I can't turn away from my new responsibility.

ABOUT THE AUTHOR

 MOLLY ZENK is a USA Today Bestselling Author who was born in Minnesota, grew up in Florida, lived in Tennessee, before settling in Colorado. She writes across genres from YA paranormal to historical to urban fantasy. Some of her recent publishing credits include: Operation Boyfriend (2019), Fierce & Fated Anthology (2019), Fated Mates Anthology (2019), the Captivity series with co-writer Sarah Biglow (2019) and United To Strike: A Novel Of The Delano Grape Workers (2019). She is married to a Mathematician/Software Engineer who complains about there not being enough "math" or info about him in her author bio. They live in Arvada, CO with their daughters.

This has been an
Immortal Production